The Vintner and The Vixen
(Vintage Love Book One)

Alexia Adams

The Vintner and The Vixen
(Vintage Love Book One)

By Alexia Adams

Published by:
Alexia Adams
Suite 377 - 255 Newport Drive
Port Moody, BC V3H 5H1
Canada

Contact: Alexia@alexia-adams.com
www.alexia-adams.com

Edited by Julie Sturgeon
Cover design by Steven Novak

e-ISBN: 978-0-9939126-1-0
Print ISBN: 978-0-9939126-4-1

First Print Edition October 2016

Dedication

To winemakers everywhere. Thank you.

Chapter 1

Jacques raked a hand through his hair then immediately pulled a comb out of his pocket and straightened the strands. *Merci à Dieu* it was Friday and he could escape from Paris to the Loire Valley. Except there he'd have to endure an entire weekend listening to his grandfather ask when he was going to marry again and continue the family name. Jacques was pretty sure his grandfather was still alive at ninety-five because he didn't trust his grandson to procreate without his continual reminders.

His phone buzzed on his desk seconds before his secretary's voice came over the intercom, starting with a giggle.

"Jacques, your grandfather is on line one, and he sounds very excited. And your brother is here—" Another giggle. Was there any woman his brother couldn't charm? Even Jacques's fifty-five-year-old, married-for-decades personal assistant was reduced to a schoolgirl when Daniel showed up.

"Send in Daniel; I'll take the call."

His younger brother strode through the door as Jacques picked up the handset. His granddad hated being on speakerphone.

"She's come," Grand-Papa said without greeting.

"Who's come?" Jacques rolled his eyes at Daniel, who lounged on the chair in front of the desk. His brother wore jeans and a white shirt with the top

1

three buttons undone. And if Jacques wasn't mistaken, and he never was, a woman's lipstick mark was under the curve of his brother's jaw. Must be nice to indulge in lovemaking in the middle of a workday. Or any day for that matter. But Daniel had never had a problem attracting the ladies. Remembering where he'd left them was another story.

"Yvette." His grandfather's voice saved him from contemplating his brother's love life. At least he had one.

"What?" He stood, and even Daniel sat up in his chair. "Grand-Papa, Daniel's here. I'm going to put you on speakerphone so we both can hear your news." He pressed the button on the phone but didn't sit back down. "Now, start at the beginning. Who has arrived?"

Jacques had been expecting this for a while, but his grandfather's mind suddenly snapping was still a shock.

"Yvette. Or rather, her great-granddaughter."

"What?" He was beginning to sound like a parrot.

"Yvette has passed and left the cottage and land to her great-granddaughter. She's come to claim it." His grandfather's voice softened as though he were explaining a difficult concept to a child.

Jacques fell into his chair. "Where is this woman now?"

"I don't think this phone is working. Or else you're not listening. I just said she's at the cottage. You are still coming home tonight, right?"

Jacques counted to ten, then backwards for good

measure. "Grand-Papa, are you saying that some girl showed up, claiming to be the great-granddaughter of a woman you haven't seen in more than seventy years, and you just let her move into the cottage?"

"Yes."

Daniel put his hand over his mouth to cover a laugh. Jacques glared at him. Didn't he realize how serious this was? Not only had a complete stranger moved into a building on their property, but she might also hold the title deed to their very best grapevines. Jacques sent an IM to his secretary, asking her to get his lawyer on the line.

"Did she have proof of ownership?"

"I don't need proof. She has Yvette's eyes."

Jacques didn't even try to stifle the groan that rose in his throat. "So, to recap, you met someone who has the same eye color as a woman you knew before 'La Vie en rose' was a hit? And that entitled this stranger to invade our estate?"

"She had a key."

Oh. That makes it all right, then.

"I'm on my way." Jacques disconnected the call and checked his watch. The next TGV train didn't depart for an hour, but the drive took two and a half—plenty of time for the thief to make off with all the antiques in the cottage. His grandfather had insisted the place remain exactly as it had been when he'd gifted it to Yvette during the Second World War. By allowing his grandfather to maintain the cottage and keep it move-in ready, Jacques had precipitated this entire event.

The only thing he could do now was get down there quickly, get rid of this woman, and make sure his grandfather had someone to keep a closer eye on him.

Jacques shoved his laptop and some papers in his briefcase.

"I've got a company car. I'll drive," Daniel said.

Jacques paused. "You know I don't like being driven."

"You want to get there today, don't you? You drive like an old lady on her way to church on Sunday."

"I drive the speed limit. Not everyone is a Formula 1 driver."

"Gotta be the best to do what I do. Jacques, if Mercedes trusts me to drive their 2.5-million-euro car, you should trust me to drive you home. Come on. I, for one, can't wait to meet this woman with the unforgettable eyes."

"Of course you can't."

As they left, Jacques's secretary transferred the lawyer through to his cell phone. But they'd already had this conversation. The property legally belonged to Yvette Tessier and formed part of her estate. The only way the de Launay family could reclaim the land was to buy it back. Maybe he should get Daniel to approach this woman on the off chance it was a relative who wanted to liquidate her assets—or had no idea what they were worth. His brother could probably get the Queen of England to sell Windsor Castle to him.

Jacques deliberately kept his eyes off the speedometer as Daniel drove. His brother made his living driving very powerful cars very, very fast. But even though he had full confidence in Daniel's ability to get them home safely, giving up control didn't sit easy with Jacques.

Daniel slowed as they wound their way through the village near the chateau. A black motorbike followed behind, inches from their back bumper. As soon as the road straightened, the bike flew by, the rider giving a jaunty wave. The scream of the engine gave even Jacques a minor thrill. Daniel sped up to keep the bike—or maybe the rider's amazing ass—in view. The biker looked back over her shoulder and then, with a burst of speed, disappeared.

They pulled into the drive just as the gates clanged closed. Someone had entered just before their arrival.

Please don't let the biker be Yvette's great-granddaughter.

"Do you want to go to the house or cottage first?" Daniel asked.

"I'll go to the cottage first, see what we're dealing with. You go to the house and check on Grand-Papa. We're going to have to talk about hiring a companion to keep an eye on him. All this being alone isn't good."

"Aye, aye, Captain."

Jacques shot him a withering glare, which just bounced off his brother's good humor. The only time Daniel was ever serious was when he was on the racetrack.

Sure enough, a black Ducati motorbike was parked beside the cottage. Just what he needed, a biker chick to deal with. He straightened his tie and was about to knock on the door when it opened.

Mon Dieu.

5

Her riding leathers were unzipped to her waist. A tiny, black crop top barely covered full breasts, and an expanse of creamy white skin disappeared beyond the zipper. But it was her halo of fiery red hair that caught his eye. It fell with abandon about her face and down her back, a single curl resting against her cleavage. She came with her own sunset.

"I thought I heard someone. You must be Charles's grandson—Jacques de Launay, isn't it?"

Damned if her voice didn't match her body, sultry and sumptuous. Her French had a Canadian accent but was perfectly understandable.

He cleared his throat. "You have me at a disadvantage. You obviously know who I am."

"And I bet you hate that, don't you?"

"Hate what?"

"That I know more about you than you do about me." She cocked a hand on her hip and the zipper pulled apart another couple centimeters, revealing more alabaster skin. Strawberries and cream. His mouth watered.

"It's not my favorite position to be in," he said.

A delighted laugh escaped her full lips. They were devoid of sticky lip gunk, perfect for kissing. He dragged his gaze from her mouth back to her smiling eyes.

"Perhaps before we discuss favorite positions, I should at least tell you my name. I'm Maya Tessier."

Her handshake was firm, and the laughter in her eyes never wavered. Jacques forced his lips to remain neutral. He wouldn't be beguiled by this woman's flirtatious attitude.

"What do you want, Ms. Tessier?"

"Call me Maya. After all, we're neighbors now."

"Over my dead body."

Her eyes raked him. "That would be a horrific waste of what appears to be a mighty fine body." This time his smile wouldn't be repressed. The women he normally associated with weren't like this—bold, brash, and hot enough to scorch the inside of an oak barrel.

The last thing he needed was to repeat his grandfather's folly and be suckered by a woman he'd never get over. *Not going to happen. Refocus, Jacques. She's just a woman out to get what she can from the family. Like all the others.*

He'd make quick work of this and get back to his relaxing weekend. Her gaze was riveted on his lips. She licked her own, and the air between them sizzled.

To hell with relaxation. Maya was a challenge he wasn't about to ignore.

***

What was it about authority that brought out the sass in her? The man before her reeked of power. Tightly controlled, highly suppressed power. Not a hair was out of place, his suit probably cost more than her bike, and despite having walked across the dusty gravel, not a speck had dared settle on his polished shoes. The whole package made her want to rumple him until he never looked pressed again.

It would be no hardship either. The man was seriously gorgeous. His eyes were the same blue as his grandfather's, his hair light brown but highlighted with blond as though he spent a lot of time outside rather than behind a desk. Either that or he had a fabulous colorist. The thought of the powerful Jacques de Launay with aluminum foil in his hair nearly set off a fit of the giggles. His full lips tightened as he continued to stare at her. Yup, authority brought out her rebellious streak. And usually got her in deep trouble. Chances were, she was heading that way now. Trouble in the guise of a sexy Frenchman.

Yes, please.

Her internal temperature went critical, and she pulled off her riding leathers to cool down. Jacques's eyes flared as he watched her undress.

"So … Maya, I imagine you are anxious to get rid of the property and return to Canada and your family." He still stood in the doorway, his head almost reaching the lintel, his shoulders nearly spanning the width. Her body hummed, but not from fear. She'd been around enough men to know which ones resorted to their fists to exert strength over a woman. Jacques would probably just kiss her into submission. *Get a grip, Maya. He's here to wheedle your inheritance out of you.* Her best plan was to knock him off balance.

"Such a vivid imagination. Surely, it could be put to better use. But to answer your question, no, I'm here to stay. Lucky for me, my father is Irish and I have the right to live in Europe. So, as I said, we're now neighbors."

"I would make you a very generous offer for the cottage and land. You could get a nice place in Paris. Surely a woman like you wants to live in the city, not be stuck out here in the countryside."

"A woman like me? Since you've known me all of two minutes, perhaps you'd like to elaborate on exactly what type of woman you think I am."

His gaze caressed her again. "You are young, beautiful, and according to your left hand, single. Paris has clubs, restaurants, shops, everything to keep you amused. I would pay you 10 million euros, and I can advise you on how to invest it so you'd never have to work again."

"That is a generous offer. However, my clubbing days are over. I prefer to eat at home. And as you can see from my wardrobe"—she gestured to her department store jeans and cotton top—"my taste in clothes is simple. Let me make myself clear, *Monsieur* de Launay. I am here to stay. Now, if you'll excuse me, I have a dinner date in half an hour and need to dress." She grabbed the door and, barely giving him time to step back, slammed it in his face.

That went well. At least it'd been the reaction she'd expected from Jacques—to try and get her off his estate right away. She had to calm down before she pitched up at his table in a few minutes. Awkward family dinners were nothing new for her. She looked forward to seeing how Jacques de Launay handled them.

Chapter 2

"She's beautiful, isn't she? The spitting image of her great-grandmother," Grand-Papa said as Jacques poured himself a drink. "When she pulled up at the gates, I thought for a second that it was my time, and I was being given a vision of Yvette before I crossed to the other side."

Grand-Papa vibrated with excitement. If Maya's arrival caused his grandfather to have a stroke, she'd find herself out on her ass before she could unpack her bags.

He handed the trusting old man a glass of wine. "Don't get too excited. She won't be here long." He sat on the sofa, hoping Grand-Papa would do the same.

"Really? When she arrived this afternoon, she said she'd come to stay."

He held back a groan of frustration. It would be hard enough to evict the woman, who technically had a legal right to the property, without his grandfather on her side. "Grand-Papa, this is our home. We can't have a stranger living in our estate. I value my privacy."

"She's not a stranger. She's Yvette's great-granddaughter."

"Remind me again why she owns the cottage." He'd only discovered that the cottage and ten hectares of their best grapes were owned by someone else when his grandfather had transferred the estate to him

10

four years ago. He'd wanted then to reclaim the property, but his grandfather had forbidden it, saying it would come back to the family in time. Well, that time was now.

Grand-Papa sighed and finally sat opposite Jacques on the replica Louis XVI fainting couch, which was about as comfortable as a cement bench. "When Yvette and I were engaged, I gave her the cottage and the land. It formed part of her estate, so when she died, Maya inherited it."

"It was a betrothal gift for a marriage that never took place. I'm sure we have a legal case to have the property restored to us. Yvette should have returned the deeds when she ran off with that other man." And it appeared Maya was just like her great-grandmother, holding onto something she had no moral right to claim.

Grand-Papa looked over Jacques's left shoulder as if he could see the past depicted on the wall behind it. "Yvette offered, and I refused."

"What?" Jacques stood.

"I hoped that one day she would return to me. But instead she sent her great-granddaughter."

Jacques would have to be careful to limit Maya's association with his grandfather, especially alone. Grand-Papa seemed to be confusing past and present. Who knew what he'd give away next?

Daniel sauntered into the room and poured himself a drink.

"Grand-Papa." Jacques forced his voice to soften. "I know you think this is some romantic movie, but the reality is that a strange woman is living a hundred meters from our house. She drives a motorbike. Who knows what kind of people she'll let in? This is unacceptable; she has to leave."

"No."

"Pardon?"

"I may no longer own this house, but I am still the Comte de Vendee and your grandfather. Maya stays for as long as she wishes. You are not to ask her to leave."

"Grand-Papa, that's too much. I can't allow it. Daniel, help me out. We can't have some wild, biker chick living on the estate."

Daniel glanced at his phone before answering. "I haven't had the pleasure of meeting the woman, and I don't discriminate based on transportation choices. You're on your own in this battle, Jacques."

Merveilleux. *I'm surrounded by romantics.*

Grand-Papa cleared his throat, a sure sign that Jacques wasn't going to like what came next. "The only other thing I've ever asked of you, Jacques, is to provide me with a great-grandchild."

"I tried." His throat tightened, and he took a sip of wine to ease the pain. *Dieu*, when would it stop hurting?

"That was three years ago. It's time you married again. Six hundred years of history are tied up in your loins. If you don't produce an heir, the de Launay name will be lost forever. We were once advisors to kings, you know. Now look at us: an old man and his business-obsessed grandson."

Daniel *not* being a de Launay was damned inconvenient. It was such a shame they shared a mother and not a father.

"My businesses allow us to keep this place. The

chateau makes no money, and the upkeep costs a fortune." And running his companies kept him sane. Kept him from remembering how empty his life was. Not everyone got to live out their dreams.

"Yes, and I'm proud of what you've accomplished. But it's time to step back from your empire and live up to your family responsibility."

Jacques clenched his teeth. Bien sûr, *I'll just pop out and impregnate the first female I come across.* He glanced up, and through the open French doors saw Maya approaching. Good thing he didn't believe in destiny.

Daniel followed his gaze. "That's the woman you want to get rid of?" Jacques nodded. "Then you'd better check your pulse, *mon frère*. I think you might be dead."

The way his blood pressure skyrocketed at the sight of Maya, death might not be far off.

***

Maya ran a damp palm down the short skirt of her dark gray dress and squared her shoulders in case anyone was watching from the huge windows of the chateau. She slowed her pace. Walking across pebbled gravel in boots was no problem. Teetering on stiletto heels was another matter. But if she was going to battle the beast on his turf, she needed every weapon in her arsenal. A dress that had brought at least one ex-boyfriend to his knees was the backup to her sharp tongue.

Be nice, Maya. You catch more flies with honey than vinegar. Although, who the hell wants to catch flies? All I want is a quiet, peaceful place to hide out and develop my art. Grace and serenity, here I come.

Jacques's grandfather, Charles, stood waiting on the back terrace, the French doors open behind him. He wore a sharp suit, complete with a rose in his buttonhole. He looked like the world's oldest prom date. But when he held out his arm to her, she took it gratefully and accompanied him into the house.

She did her best not to gawk like a commoner at the room's outrageously flamboyant style. God, there was enough gold paint in here to cover the dome of Les Invalides in Paris. For a house not open to the public, they might have updated the decor a little. After a quick look around the room, she dared a glance at its owner. Jacques lounged on a sofa, a glass of red wine in his hand. His eyes narrowed, and his lips held a firm line. She sent him her best smile, followed by a little wink when he shifted uncomfortably.

A rich, male laugh brought her eyes around to a man she hadn't noticed. Although how she could have missed such an incredible specimen of manhood, she didn't know. Her womanly instincts were way off. Or too consumed with the cold and controlled Jacques. The new guy looked vaguely familiar; she'd concentrated so much on researching Jacques, she hadn't thought to check for other relatives.

"*Bon soir*, Maya. Welcome to Chateau de Vendee. I am Daniel Michaud, Jacques's younger half brother," he said as he glided over to her. Standing before her was every girl's fantasy: Formula 1's current champion and world-class playboy. So why did her eyes travel back to the reserved older brother?

It was rumored that Daniel's races lasted longer than his relationships. But she still felt nothing. Not even a flicker of lust when his stunning green eyes roved over her. Yet every cell in her body lit up when Jacques's gaze traveled the length of her bare legs. It didn't matter. A relationship with either man would be suicide. Both were too involved in the media and their careers. Her life depended on her staying in the shadows, hidden in her little cottage behind Jacques's massive gates.

Daniel kissed her on both cheeks in greeting, and from the corner of her eye she saw Jacques sit up straighter. Charles handed her a wineglass, and she took a tentative sip. The rich, red wine teased her taste buds. She was normally more a beer or Jack Daniel's drinker, but this wine had the potential to convert her. She'd never had anything so velvety.

"Thank you. You have all been so welcoming." She glanced again at Jacques, who raised his wineglass in mock salute.

"Would you like a tour of the house before dinner?" Charles asked. Maya forced her gaze from Jacques to the older man.

"Yes, I'd love to see it," she said.

"Perhaps Daniel could take you," Charles suggested.

Daniel smiled. Jacques's mouth tightened even more.

"If Daniel gives me the tour, I have a feeling I'll end up in some dark corner being seduced by my guide. I've made that mistake before."

15

"I'm a fantastic mistake." Daniel flashed another of his sexy grins, but it just bounced off her.

"I don't doubt it. But I'm looking to learn from my bad decisions, not upgrade them," she replied.

Jacques laughed, and the sound set off a fluttery feeling in her chest. "She has your measure, Daniel. At last, a woman who can resist your charm."

"I am cut through the heart," Daniel said as he pulled an imaginary knife out of his chest.

"Hardly." She immediately liked Daniel; he was easy-going with a playful side. Normally she'd enjoy flirting and bantering with him. But her senses were too attuned to every move his older brother made. Maybe because Jacques was her opposite, he drew her like a magnet. "Would you show me your home, Jacques?"

He stood and Maya swallowed. Even with her being five feet, eight inches, and wearing four-inch heels, he towered over her. He had to be six foot four, at least. Her heart rate accelerated and her mouth went dry.

"It would be my pleasure."

The way he said pleasure sent a shiver down her spine. Perhaps she was safer with Daniel after all. But she'd issued the challenge. There was no going back now.

Jacques held out his arm and Maya placed her hand tentatively on it. Even at home he looked like he was about to chair a board meeting, although she felt the corded muscles beneath the super-soft material of his suit. As soon as they were out of the room, she let go.

He led her into a hallway wide enough to drive a

16

car down. A thick wool rug covered the marble tiles and muffled their footsteps. Where on earth did you get a runner fifty feet long? Certainly not at Ikea, where she bought the bulk of her furnishings.

"So, you don't think I'm capable of luring a woman into a dark corner and seducing her?" His voice lowered, and the heat in his gaze made her wish she'd worn a short-sleeved dress.

"I didn't think you'd be interested."

"You are a beautiful woman in a dress that demands attention. I am a man. Seduction is always in the cards."

"Just because you're powerful and rich doesn't mean I'm going to fall into your bed."

"You wouldn't fall in—I'd carry you. But I thought you wanted the tour first."

So, he thought he could get her in bed with just the crook of his little finger, eh? Arrogant bastard. And damn the warmth flooding her system at the idea that he'd want her there.

He opened one half of a double door that led into a room at the front of the house. The fifteen-foot high windows let in loads of light, even so late in the evening. The last rays of sunshine bounced off the mirrors and gold-painted furniture almost blindingly.

"Wow," she said, struggling to keep the sarcasm out of her voice.

"Yes, I know." Jacques let out a sigh. "My wife decorated when I was away on business for six weeks."

His wife? She checked his left hand, which still held his wineglass. Yup, golden ring on the fourth finger. Rookie mistake, Maya. Always check the marital status first. He thought she'd fall into his bed with his wife already there? Jerk. It was the giant stop sign her body needed, and she put another foot of distance between them.

"I'm sure on less sunny days it's not so ... overwhelming."

"It's horrible. But I haven't had the time to supervise a redecoration."

"What about your wife?" For all her Internet research, she hadn't read about Jacques's personal life. In fact, every report had been about his business accomplishments, so she'd assumed he wasn't married.

Jacques blinked, but his voice remained calm. "She's dead."

"I'm so sorry." Maybe that was why he was so stiff and formal—he was still grieving for his wife. "The furniture's not bad; it fits with the room. It just needs toning down. Reupholster the chairs in cream or some pale color, return the wood to anything other than gold, rearrange the artwork, reposition the mirrors so they don't blind you when you walk in..." She stopped talking. Her vision for the room's potential had captured her imagination. But he probably wasn't yet ready to let go of his wife's stamp on the house, atrocious as it was.

He turned the full intensity of his gaze on her. "Interesting ideas. Are you an interior decorator?"

"No, I'm an artist. Well, that's what I want to be. Up to now I've paid the bills by working in a club and doing other things. But in addition to the cottage, Gran-Gran left me a little money, so I'm hoping to concentrate on my art for as long as the money lasts."

Again his intense gaze sent shivers up and down her spine, and the room seemed to shrink in size and cocoon around them. She took another sip of her wine to relieve the dryness in her mouth.

"Let's continue the tour. Or would you rather I moved on to the seduction?" He raised his eyebrows and she laughed. God, he was gorgeous when he wasn't being such a prick. Considering her past was littered with jerks, she usually had well-honed defenses. With a single laugh, he'd destroyed them. Jacques was dangerous.

They looked into a few other rooms, all of them inelegantly decorated. They wandered down another hallway, this one lined with portraits of de Launays long dead. Maya, interested in the different artistic techniques used over the years, stopped to examine a couple of the paintings. Jacques stood quietly beside her, answering her questions politely but otherwise not disturbing her concentration. Yet she was aware of his body close to hers. When he took a step to the side, she missed the warmth and followed him automatically.

At last they arrived at the portrait of Charles. His blue eyes lacked the mischief she'd seen in them today, and although he had a ring on his left hand, there was no joy in his face. The last painting was of a man who bore more than a passing resemblance to Jacques.

"My father," he said quietly. "He was killed in a plane crash when I was eight."

"I'm sorry. Is your mother still alive?"

"Yes, but she lives in Paris and never comes here. She and my father were separated even before

his death, so my grandfather raised Daniel and me."
Again his tone was unemotional, as though everyone
was abandoned by their mother in early childhood.
But he'd returned to being stiff and unapproachable.

"Why is there no portrait of you?"

"The tradition is for the man to have his picture
painted after he has produced an heir. It is highly
likely that my father's portrait will be the last of the
de Launays to hang in this hallway."

Her argument shriveled on her tongue at the
fierce look in his eyes. Either he was still so in love
with his wife that he couldn't contemplate
remarrying, or the marriage had been such a disaster
that he wouldn't go there again.

Why should she care which it was?

Chapter 3

Jacques gripped his wineglass tighter and shoved his free hand into his pocket to keep from touching Maya's bare back. *Merde*, to keep from touching any part of her. The woman was seriously compelling, and ever since her quip about seduction, he hadn't been able to think of anything else. Although with Maya, it was more likely to be a conflagration than a seduction.

How could a woman look so sexy wearing gray? A person who wants to blend into the background wears gray. A super-hot twenty-something with an ass that could make an atheist rethink the existence of a benevolent creator does not. Gray, however, was the perfect backdrop for her molten hair. And her legs? Did they never end? He was used to looking down at his female companions. Maya was right up there with him. And rather than stoop or try to minimize her size as he'd seen other tall women do, she walked with an attitude that said, *I'm here. Deal with it.*

But all her beautiful packaging was eclipsed by her eyes. He had to admit, his grandfather was right. A man didn't forget eyes like that, not while he was still breathing, anyway. They were the color of cognac. Not the first glass, the one you sipped as you wondered when your day had gone from all right to complete shit. Maya's eyes were the color of the third glass, the one you stared into and for a brief moment

it reflected all your hopes and dreams back at you—
seconds before you slung it down your throat and
went to bed. Alone.

A distant chime made Maya turn in the direction
of the sound.

"What's that?" Her voice was huskier than usual.
A faint blush stained her cheeks. Was she turned on
by him? Or the house? She was already redecorating
in her mind. Was she planning on upgrading from the
cottage to the chateau? He could certainly imagine
her decorating his bedroom. And it wouldn't involve
a can of paint.

"Dinner bell. Are you hungry?"

"Starving." Her gaze roved over him again. This
woman wasn't shy, and her boldness, rather than
putting him off, ignited an answering passion in him.
Maya Tessier was potent.

"Let's get you fed, then."

When they arrived at the dining room, Daniel
and Grand-Papa were already seated next to each
other. Which left the two chairs opposite for him and
Maya. Since his father's death, when it was just the
family to dine, no one sat at the head of the table.
Grand-Papa clearly considered Maya family and
hadn't adjusted the seating. He helped her into the
chair across from his grandfather, forcing his eyes
away from the extra two inches of thigh exposed
when she sat. Jacques swallowed. This was going to
be a hell of a long dinner.

"So, Maya, tell us about yourself," Grand-Papa
said as the first course was being served.

"Not much to tell. I was born in British
Columbia on the west coast of Canada. After I

finished high school, I went to live with my great-grandmother in Montreal. There I went to art school and did various jobs to help support myself. Before she died, Gran-Gran made me promise to come to France and focus on my art for at least a year, so she left the cottage and land to me in her will. And here I am." From the way she fidgeted with her cutlery, Jacques could see there was way more to Maya's story than she was telling.

"You intend to stay only for the year, then?" Jacques seized upon the idea. He could resist her for a year. Couldn't he? That was fifty-two weekends, less if he stayed in Paris for a few of those. That was survivable. Then Maya took a deep breath, which drew his eyes to her chest. And he wasn't sure he could make it through the next two days.

"We'll see. I quit my job and sold the apartment where Gran-Gran and I lived. I have nothing and no one to go back to."

"What about your family?" Charles asked.

"I haven't lived with my parents for almost ten years, so we've grown apart. My twin brother is married and has his own life…" Her voice trailed off and she took a sip of her wine.

"Their loss is our gain," Daniel said.

Jacques shot him a warning glare, but it only made his brother laugh.

"When is your next race?" Maya asked Daniel.

"Not until the middle of August. We're on summer break for another two weeks."

The rest of the meal passed in a discussion of Daniel's racing career, the upcoming grape harvest, and various other banalities. By the time the serving staff placed the cheese and fruit on the table for the last course, Maya lounged back in her chair, sipping her second glass of wine, looking like she came to dinner every night. At some point she'd kicked off her shoes, and her bare foot had come perilously close to rubbing against his calf on several occasions. Only ten minutes after the meal, he couldn't remember a single thing he'd eaten.

"I am sorry, but my age is showing," Grand-Papa said. "I am tired and must go to bed. Thank you for joining us for dinner, Maya. I hope this is the first of many meals you will share with us. *Bonne nuit*."

"I'll see you to your room, Grand-Papa," Daniel said. "I've got some emails to answer and meetings to set up, so I'll say good night as well. It was a pleasure to meet you, Maya. As Grand-Papa said, I hope this is just the first meal you share with us. It's way more enjoyable to stare at you across the table than my old brother."

Maya laughed and the sound trickled down Jacques's spine. She stood and strode around the table, barefoot, and kissed his grandfather on the cheek. "Good night, Charles. Sleep well. Will you come to the cottage, or shall I meet you here for our date tomorrow?"

Grand-Papa's eyes had a definite mischievous twinkle as he glanced at Jacques. "Would you come here? It's such a long walk to the cottage."

Since when? It was a hundred meters, and Grand-Papa walked the gardens daily, plus he had a golf cart for getting around when his knees bothered him. What game was the old man playing now?

"Do I get a kiss?" Daniel asked.

"I think you've had your quota for the day," Maya replied. She reached out and wiped off the lipstick stain from under Daniel's jaw with her thumb.

Daniel and his grandfather left, and Jacques stared at Maya from across the table. He had to keep her away from his grandfather. Grand-Papa had always had a weakness for beautiful women, as evidenced by the situation they were in now. Jacques wouldn't allow Maya to take further advantage of his grandfather's trusting nature—or his own apparent penchant for sexy redheads. In answer to Daniel's earlier observation, no, he wasn't dead. But that didn't mean he was going to be ruled by his body.

"Do you wish for something else? A coffee, perhaps?" Jacques offered to take his mind off kissing her. He definitely hadn't had his quota today.

"No, I'm good. In fact, I'd better get to bed, too."

Want company? He managed to stop himself from blurting it out. *Maudit*, the woman eroded his control.

"I'll just get my shoes," she said as she dropped to her knees.

"Allow me." He pulled back his chair and kneeled to find her footwear. They both reached for the same shoe from opposite sides of the table.

Maya's laugh reverberated off the underside of the table and did wicked things to his body. "We meet again, Monsieur de Launay," she said in a seductive tone.

He pushed both shoes towards her and scooted out from under the table before his control completely snapped.

"I'll walk you to the cottage." His voice was harsh as he wrestled with the desire to push her back under the table, slide the dress from her body, and make love to her until the chandelier shook.

She sat on his grandfather's chair as she slipped her shoes back on. "There's no need. I'm only in the backyard. And your impressive gates prevent strangers from getting in." Was she referring to the gates at the drive or the reserved demeanor he projected to keep people from getting close?

"I am a gentleman. And a gentleman always sees a lady home after dinner."

"I hate to break it to you, but I'm no lady. And calling yourself a gentleman is a challenge to me."

"A challenge?" He walked around the table and helped her to her feet. They stood so close, he could feel her breath as she released a sigh.

"Makes me want to push your buttons until I find the one that turns you from gentleman to wild man. Can't help it, I'm a rebel at heart."

Chérie, *you've already found that button. Now I have to stop you from pushing it.*

***

The cool night air blew across Maya's overheated skin and she shivered. Jacques immediately shrugged out of his jacket and put it around her shoulders.

"Thank you," she murmured. His cologne lingered on the jacket, and the spicy scent made her head swim.

He'd snagged a flashlight from the house before they'd left, and he kept the path in front of her feet illuminated. While he lit the way, she searched her overwhelmed brain for a topic of conversation. And came up blank. Evidently Jacques de Launay had shut her up. A first for her.

When they got closer to the cottage, she noticed the light on in her bedroom. The sun had still been up when she'd left, so she hadn't bothered turning on any lights, not even the one for outside. A shiver wracked her body that even Jacques's jacket couldn't prevent.

Had they found her? She tripped, and his arm came around her waist to steady her.

"Are you okay?" His deep voice helped hold back the panic threatening to seize her.

"There's a light on in my room. I'm pretty sure I didn't leave it on," she said, her gaze riveted on her window. Not even her brother knew where she was. And Jacques had those huge gates; surely they'd keep most people out. But Big Tony wasn't most people.

Jacques's arm tightened around her. "The lights may be on a timer. But I'll check to make sure it's safe." He took the key from her hand and unlocked the door.

She wanted to be independent and stand on her own. But she also wanted to live another day. "If you don't mind."

"It would be my pleasure," he said, his voice low and sexy.

That pulled a smile from her. "We really need to discuss your idea of pleasure," she replied.

His eyes widened before a grin curved his lips. "I'm going into your bedroom."

"Alone."

"For now." Without waiting for her reply, he strode through to the kitchen and up the narrow stairs to the rooms above. When he hadn't returned after a minute, she followed. He was probably riffling through her things, looking for some angle to get her off his property. If he knew of the danger she was in…

She found him in her room, staring at her bed. Was there some kind of message there? A warning of what was to come? God, if it were a horse's head, she'd throw up. She grabbed Jacques's arm as she peered around his large form. There on her bed, flung across the spread, lay her black nightie. Right where she'd left it when she'd quickly unpacked this afternoon. Relief swept through her.

Her eyes darted to Jacques's face; he blinked and then swallowed. *Shaken by lingerie, good to know.*

"You seem to be safe. Lock the door behind me when I leave."

"Thank you." Their gazes locked, and the desire in his blue eyes set off an answering hunger within her. She wasn't going to win this game without keeping him off balance. "Don't you want your goodnight kiss?" *Way to play with fire, Maya.*

"No." He fled her bedroom.

She went downstairs to lock the door. As the bolt clicked into the frame she heard him say, "*Bonne nuit*," through the door.

The chances of her having a good night when her brain was full of Jacques were pretty slim.

Do not try to escape one man by getting lost in the arms of another.

Chapter 4

Maya woke to a pounding on her front door. She opened one eye and squinted at the clock. It was 7:00 a.m. On a Saturday. Someone was about to die.

She grabbed her wrap as the pounding continued, tying it as she raced down the stairs. There was no peephole, and given her state of undress, she called through the closed door, "Who is it? And I only ask so I know what name to give the paramedics when I beat you senseless for waking me at this hour."

A masculine chuckle was followed by Jacques's deep voice. "I come with coffee. And pastries."

She opened the door a crack and peeked through. Any other man showing up at a woman's door with coffee would carry it in two paper cups. Not Jacques. No, he held a tray with a silver coffee carafe, two porcelain gold-rimmed cups, and cream and sugar in tiny silver pots. The aroma of fresh coffee wafted over to her. A basket covered with a lace-edged tea towel hung from the crook of his elbow. It was that, and not the sexy smile, that made her open the door wide.

"You should thank your chef. Pastries saved your life this morning," she said, gesturing for him to enter.

Jacques hesitated for a second then stepped into the cottage. He cleared his throat. "I'll be sure to thank him. I'll set up breakfast in the kitchen while you get dressed."

"Don't you like what I'm wearing?" Who knew she was such a pyromaniac, always playing with fire?

"Too much. Get dressed, Maya. In twenty minutes there will be a half dozen men here to install a security system. If you're still wearing that, I may never be able to get them to leave."

She scurried up the stairs, returning ten minutes later in an aqua-colored crop top and white jean shorts. She'd pulled her hair into a messy bun at her nape, brushed her teeth quickly, and applied a coat of mascara. The man had brought pastries, after all. He deserved something decent to look at while he ate them.

When she returned to the kitchen, Jacques had breakfast set up on the small table. The back door was open to let in the fresh morning air. He stood gazing out the doorway, and she took the opportunity to stare at him. He'd replaced yesterday's suit with lightweight, tan pants and a short-sleeved blue shirt. The latter was stretched tight across his back and shoulders. And when he bent over to toss a bit of bread to an animal outside, she was able to appreciate his other fine assets. He turned around at her audible intake of breath.

His gaze ran over her, lingering on her exposed midriff and belly button ring. The temperature in the kitchen ratcheted up a couple more degrees.

"Don't you have any clothes that cover your whole body?" he asked.

She shrugged. She didn't dress to please a man. It was warm, and she wanted to be comfortable. "Not at the moment." Taking a seat at the table, she poured them both a coffee and added a spoonful of sugar to hers. Still he stared. She shifted in her chair. Who was off balance now?

"How did you get a crew to install the security system on such short notice—and on a Saturday?" Was he going to change the access code the minute her back was turned so she couldn't get in? She had the law on her side; the deed to the cottage was safely locked away. But she couldn't risk going to court and making the whole dispute public. So she'd let him think he was winning. For now.

"I'm Jacques de Launay. When I pick up the phone, people come running." He sipped his coffee and continued to stare at her over the rim.

She was used to male attention. Hell, she'd worked as a nude model at her art school to pay for some of her classes. And not a night went by at the club without at least three propositions. But the look in Jacques's eyes was different.

"That easy? Must be nice."

"Most of the time." He handed her the basket of pastries, and she selected a *pain au chocolat*, her favorite. "I can see that if the security people are going to finish today, I'll have to keep you away from here. Would you like a tour of the estate?"

"Is that some sort of veiled insult?"

"No, it's a compliment on your ability to distract even the most determined of men." Was he referring to himself? Surely the great Jacques de Launay had more to do on his Saturday than escort an improperly dressed Canadian girl around his estate.

"I'm supposed to meet with your grandfather at ten."

He pulled apart a croissant. "Consider me as his

stand-in. I left him a note saying you'd be with me today."

"That was presumptuous of you."

"I prefer the term *self-assured*. It makes me sound less obnoxious."

"If you say so." But she did want to see her inheritance. "Will you show me the ten hectares I own?"

His mouth tightened. "We need to discuss that. The land is an integral part of the winery and the whole estate. You must sell it back to the family."

"I *must* do nothing." She put down her cup and crossed her arms.

"Are you always this disagreeable?"

"Always. Still want to show me your estate?"

He sighed, although it was accompanied by a wicked smile. "I can see no other way."

"Bite me."

"With pleasure."

Before he could take up her challenge, the sound of vehicles at the front of the cottage announced the arrival of the security system people. Jacques rose and went to the door, and she followed after popping the last bit of croissant into her mouth. He greeted each of the workers with a handshake and asked the name of the two he didn't already seem to know. A man who took time for the little people—perhaps he wasn't so bad after all.

"When will you be ready to go?" Jacques asked after he introduced her to the lead man. Workers were already swarming all over the cottage.

"Five minutes," she replied, hurrying to the bathroom before that, too, was invaded. It was going to take a hell of a lot longer than five minutes to prepare herself for a day in the company of Jacques de Launay.

***

Jacques put the milk in Maya's fridge and the remaining pastries in her bread box while she finished getting ready. Grand-Papa may have prohibited him from kicking Maya out of the cottage, but he hadn't said anything about getting the land back. If Maya didn't return the ten hectares his grandfather had so foolishly gifted to the woman who had stolen his heart, then the winery would go under. The key for Jacques would be to keep his focus on business and off Maya's body.

Dieu, when she'd appeared in that sexy top and those ass-hugging shorts … this day was going to test his restraint to the limit. He pulled out his wallet and the sonogram photo he kept there. It had been folded and unfolded to the point of ripping, the picture faded by the heat from his body. It didn't matter; the image was etched in his heart. When he'd been given the picture of his son, everything had seemed right in his world for the first time. Now it was a reminder of why he couldn't get involved with another woman. Ever.

By the time Maya returned, he had himself under control. She'd slipped on a pair of canvas shoes and had a small backpack slung over her shoulder.

"Ready?" he asked.

"Almost." She strode over to him, reached up, and ran her hands through his hair. Shock rooted him to the spot. "There, that's better," she said as she stepped back, her head cocked to one side. "I can't spend the day with a man whose hair looks better than mine." Her smile left him like a deer in the headlights. *Merde*.

He resisted the urge to smooth his hair back into place. If being a bit disheveled was what it took to get on Maya's good side, he could play along. It had nothing whatsoever to do with the fact that the feel of her fingers on his scalp lingered, sending tingles down his spine. If he was as smart as people said he was, he'd introduce Maya to his estate manager and head back to Paris, find the first available woman in his address book, and forget Maya Tessier even existed. But he couldn't leave his grandfather vulnerable to this woman's charms.

He steered her towards the underground garage, the doorway cleverly concealed in some shrubbery.

"Are you taking me somewhere they'll never find my body?" she asked as he opened the door and gestured for her to precede him. Her body was tense, her eyes wary.

"No. This is where we park the cars. We may be at odds about your inheritance, but I would never hurt you."

She searched his face. "Why is your car down here?" She walked down the cement steps, her light scent lingering behind her.

"One problem with owning a sixteenth-century house is that the original builders forgot to leave a place for parking. And the French Heritage Society wouldn't let us put up another building on the grounds, so we went underneath the rose garden."

"Clever." She looked around at the assortment of super-cars. "Whoa. This place would make Iron Man rust with envy."

"Most of these are Daniel's. He's the car buff. We can take one of them if you prefer. He won't mind. I have the Land Rover and the BMW; my Audi is in Paris."

"Whatever you want."

"If we take the Land Rover, we can go off road. There's a little lake where I thought we could have a picnic lunch."

"Sounds perfect."

He pulled a set of keys out of the lock box and opened the vehicle so she could get in. As she settled into the seat, wiggling her bottom as if to embed herself, he was surprised at how much he was looking forward to spending the day with Maya.

When they arrived at the winery building, Maya hopped out of the vehicle without waiting for him to open her door. Out of the air conditioning, the day was becoming very warm. Maya, however, looked delectably cool, and he had to force his hand from touching the bare skin at her waist.

"Wow, it's hot," she said as she pulled the elastic out of her low ponytail and refastened it near her crown, revealing a tattoo on the back of her neck. He took a step closer to read the intricate script.

"Grace and serenity?" They weren't the first two words that came to mind when he thought of Maya. Those were *sexy* and *trouble*.

She laughed. Definitely sexy trouble. "That was my great-grandmother's catch phrase. She said you can't control what life throws at you, but you can control your reaction. If you deal with adversity with grace and serenity, then nothing can ever keep you down. I probably should have had the tattoo on my forehead though, as my reaction is more often anger and denial."

"Your great-grandmother sounds like an interesting woman."

"She was incredible. I wish I were half the woman she was at my age. By the time Gran-Gran was twenty-six, she'd already lived through a war, been married and abandoned, and had a three-year-old daughter. All I've done is get in a load of trouble, definitely without grace or serenity." Her eyes went from liquid cognac to solid amber.

"I have a feeling your time will come. The war made people grow up faster. Why didn't your great-grandmother return to France after her husband left? She had family here, didn't she?"

"Gran-Gran said she'd made her choice and had to live with it. Your grandfather was married. And she couldn't live near him and not be with him."

"She left Grand-Papa for another man two weeks before their wedding. I don't think she could have loved him that much."

"And your grandfather married some other woman two weeks later. He couldn't have been that heartbroken either."

"There was no love in my grandfather's marriage. I think he married to hide his shame at being left by Yvette. My grandmother died before I was born, but not even my father had fond memories of her."

"I'm sorry to hear that. Gran-Gran wasn't happy

either. My great-grandfather was a drinker and a gambler. He lost all his money and then ran away, leaving his wife and newborn child destitute."

"Sounds like your great-grandmother got what she deserved."

If looks were poison, he would have been writhing on the ground in his death throes.

"No one deserves to be abandoned. She made a mistake—chose the wrong man. She let love blind her to great-grandfather's real nature. It happens all the time."

"Are you speaking from personal experience?"

A shadow crossed Maya's eyes. *Maudit*, he was supposed to convince her to sell the land back to him, not delve into her past. The truth was, Yvette had taken advantage of his grandfather's gentle heart. Jacques had to get back the property that rightfully belonged to his family.

"The women in my family are crap at choosing men. It's almost as if someone cursed us to marry losers once Gran-Gran left Charles."

"I don't believe in curses. But I do believe in trust. Once that is broken, it can never be repaired. And that's one thing a marriage should have—trust."

"Not love?"

He laughed, but there was no humor in it. When had the pleasant day turned into a soul-baring interrogation? "Love is for romance books and pop songs. I prefer to live in reality."

"I'm not so sure I like your reality. What's your problem? Did your wife cheat on you or something?"

"Or something."

"And that's it? You give up on love because one

woman didn't live up to your ideal of what a wife should be? I think maybe you need to let it go and lighten up."

The coffee is his stomach began to boil. "Lighten up? Perhaps you think I should be more like my wife? Clarisse thought only of herself and having fun. She was reckless and irresponsible and ended up killing not only herself but my unborn child as well."

Bile rose in his throat and he strode through the winery doors, not caring if Maya followed or not. Why the hell had he told her that? He couldn't bear to live through the memory again. Clarisse had been texting, driving too fast, and not wearing her seat belt when she died. And he'd been the one to find her mangled body. He'd looked into her dead eyes and realized he'd never hold the son he'd been so excited about. Her irresponsibility had been the ultimate betrayal.

Maya grabbed his arm, put one hand on his face, and with her unforgettable eyes gazed into his. "I'm so sorry, Jacques. Not only for my words but for your loss. I can't imagine what it must feel like to lose a child. If you want to cancel the tour and take me home, I completely understand." Her voice was soft, caring.

It was the out he'd wanted. He could go back to the chateau, or better yet, return to Paris and forget all about the woman with the cognac eyes. So why did his chest tighten at the thought of not spending the rest of the day with her?

"No, I want to show you why it's important that you sell the land back to me," he said.

Merveilleux, *now I've started lying to myself.*

38

This was going to end in disaster.

Chapter 5

After a tour of the winery and a brief stop to see her grapes—which looked like the million others around her—Jacques pulled up next to a picturesque lake, not a soul in sight. It was surrounded by terraces of vines; a few tall trees provided shade, but it was the view of the chateau in the distance that really sold the scene. It was the perfect location for a period film.

"This place is stunning. How come we're the only ones here? A beautiful day like today? I'm surprised it's not crowded."

"It's private property. My property."

"Damn, man. You have it all, don't you?"

"Not everything," he replied. He grabbed a blanket off the backseat and passed it to her. "Can you spread this out? I'll get the food."

She took the blanket and wandered over to the lakeshore. What was she doing here? The gangster's girlfriend and the billionaire. She needed to shatter the romantic mood before it sucked her in. The best way she knew to do that? Bring up the exes.

"I bet you and your wife came here all the time," she said as she placed the blanket on the ground. The grass was salted with tiny daisies.

"Clarisse thought eating on the ground was for the poor. And if there wasn't wait staff to cater to her every whim, she wasn't interested."

"Oh." Mission accomplished—Maya no longer felt romantic. As the silence lengthened, she tried again. She needed Jacques to accept her living in the cottage; she had nowhere else to go. "How about when you were a kid? Did you come here often then?"

"Daniel and I used to fish in the lake. And he used to bring girlfriends here. He was the one who suggested it as a good picnic spot."

"So while Daniel was romancing the girls, what were you doing?"

He placed the picnic hamper on the edge of the blanket. The first thing he pulled out was a bottle of wine and two glasses. Not the plastic kind with the removable bottom that most people used when they went on picnics. No, Jacques had real crystal with gold leaf around the rim. He poured her a glass, taking his time with her question.

"I was studying and hanging around the winery. Daniel's always been the ladies' man."

"Maybe, but I don't think you did too badly. You have that whole brooding, tortured hero thing down pat. I'm sure you were beating the girls off in school. Or did you go to one of those all-boys schools?"

"No, we went to the local school. After my father died and *Maman* remarried, Grand-Papa wanted to keep us at home so we didn't feel abandoned. And he didn't hold with rich kids going to school only with rich kids. He said we'd never learn to interact with everyday people. Anytime we pretended we were better because we lived in the big house, he'd make us spend the day with the staff, doing their bidding." He handed her a china plate and real silver cutlery. Picnics de Launay style were a whole 'nother level.

"Your grandfather is amazing." His eyes flashed

a warning she didn't understand. What, did he think she was going to seduce his grandfather? She'd done a lot of things in her life, but she was no Anna Nicole Smith.

"He's pretty special. And even though Daniel isn't technically his grandson, he never treated him any differently from me. What about your family? You mention your great-grandmother frequently but not your parents or grandparents."

Jacques placed a container with tiny appetizer bites between them. Each one looked like a miniature work of art. She picked up a few and put them on her plate, arranging them into an empty square. If he knew why she'd really moved into the cottage, he'd definitely have a fit about security. But even her brother didn't know where she was living now. He had only a phone number.

"My parents are okay. Opposite spectrum to your family. They live in a trailer park on a piece of land prone to flooding. My dad is a deadbeat, and my mother works two jobs. I have a twin brother; he's a teacher—one of those they make movies about. Always trying to save the kids in trouble, running youth programs, trying to get the druggies to turn to sports to get their kicks, that sort of thing."

"And your grandparents?"

"I never met my dad's parents. Dad emigrated from Ireland when he was twenty, and they died when I was young. And my mother's mother is a hippie; not sure who my grandfather is on that side. She lives in a commune. Last time I saw my grandmother, she was going through a nudist phase. Let's just say it was a very short visit and I haven't been back since."

He nearly choked on his canapé. "And do nudist tendencies run in your family?"

"I refuse to answer that question," she replied with a laugh. "Just make sure you knock when you come to the cottage." This was better; if she could make him laugh, maybe he wouldn't try to get rid of her. Maybe they could even be friends. Then he looked at her with those gorgeous blue eyes. Nope, she could never be *just friends* with this man.

"We'll see. At dinner, you said you went to live with your great-grandmother when you finished school. Why didn't you stay nearer your parents?"

She shifted and stared at the lake for a moment. "The art schools in Montreal are better. And Gran-Gran was getting old and needed someone nearby."

He paused for minute; hopefully, the interrogation was over. Then he asked, "Why do you have your great-grandmother's maiden name and not your father's?"

She popped a canapé into her mouth to buy time. "I got into a bit of trouble, and the best way to distance myself from that seemed to be to change my name." Too bad it hadn't worked.

He stared at her a moment but thankfully let the topic drop. "What kind of art do you do?"

At last—something she could talk about for hours without incriminating herself. "So far, mostly painting and some sculpting with clay. But I'm hoping to do some larger pieces, maybe with wood when I get a chance. I'd love to paint you. You have a very interesting face."

He pulled out another container, this one had a

green salad with tiny strips of steak. As he lifted the lid, the aroma of garlic and spices tickled her nose.

"As interesting as my face may be, I'm sure you can find a worthier subject to paint. Would you like more wine?"

That was the politest rebuff she'd ever received. But she was sure she could paint him from memory. Every time his lips twitched upward, her blood rushed a bit faster around her body. Maybe she should bring up her exes to kill the mood again. But which one? The murdered one? The one doing twenty years for murdering someone else? Or the one who'd used her to get into an organized crime ring and then dumped her when he'd achieved his goal? She was definitely skilled at picking losers.

Perhaps a neutral topic of conversation would be better. "Can you tell me about the history of the chateau? Did anyone important live there?"

"Aside from the current residents?" He laughed, and the deep rumble set off an avalanche of sensation inside her. But at least the history lesson kept them going through the rest of the delicious meal.

She was lying back on the blanket, watching the clouds drift by, when he said, "Maya, we have to discuss the land you own. We've been maintaining the vines for the past seventy years. If we hadn't cared for them, they would be worthless now. The grapes you own are critical to the success of the winery. They're a special varietal we haven't been able to successfully grow elsewhere on the estate. Without them, our product is mediocre to say the least. And I won't put out a mediocre product. My grandfather gave the best to your great-grandmother.

We must have it back to keep the winery profitable. At least fifty people depend on it for employment."

Although he laid out a compelling argument, the underlining tone was, *You have no choice. Give me back what's rightfully mine.* Well, she did have a choice, and a title deed. But she also had security issues, so she needed to tread carefully.

"I'm not selling, Jacques. But as I can't possibly eat ten hectares of wine grapes, I'll let you use them to make your wine. Despite what you may think, I haven't come to destroy your family, or the winery. I just want to start over and work on my art."

"That's not an answer I can accept."

She sat up. "Tough. It's the only answer you're going to get. If these grapes are so important, why didn't you contact my gran-gran years ago and try to get her to sell? I'm sure you checked her out; you knew she wasn't rich. If you'd have made her an offer…" Would Gran-Gran have taken the money? She'd been so adamant that Maya not sell, maybe Jacques had been in contact before.

"My grandfather insisted that I leave things as they were. Out of respect for him, I did so, even though I hated leaving the issue unresolved."

"Well, after all this time, one more year won't make any difference."

"So you'll return the land next year?"

"I'll look at all my options next year." *If I'm still alive.* She didn't need the land, but knowing how desperate Jacques was for it, she now had some bargaining power if things went sideways.

He tightened his lips but said nothing more. They packed up their lunch and headed back to the Land

Rover. Maya bundled the blanket in the backseat and stood by the door as Jacques returned the picnic basket to the trunk.

The peacefulness of the spot had been ruined by their argument. Next time, she'd come alone and bring her sketchbook. Or she'd come early with her paints and a canvas and capture the sunrise over the chateau. She was so intent on studying the scene before her, she didn't notice Jacques standing next to her until he spoke.

"What now? Thinking of upgrading from the cottage to the chateau?"

She ran a hand over the back of her neck. *Grace and serenity*. Here goes nothing. "Jacques, I don't want to fight with you. Can we call a truce? For your grandfather's sake?"

"How's this armistice supposed to work?" His eyes were riveted on her lips.

She lowered her chin, forcing his gaze to hers. "You carry on like I'm not here and don't mention me selling the cottage and land. And I work on my art and stay out of your way."

"I foresee one problem with that plan."

"What's that?"

"You're not a woman I can ignore."

"I'm not?"

"Nope. Even angry at your refusal to sell, I still want to kiss you."

"You didn't want to last night."

"Last night I was laboring under the false impression that I can resist you."

"You need to work on that." Great, now her voice was all breathy, like she wanted him to kiss her

46

or something.

"Believe me, I'm trying. But you have a spot of chocolate on the corner of your mouth, and all I can think about is licking it off."

She lifted her hand to remove the chocolate but found it trapped between their bodies as he pulled her against him. His head descended, and his tongue removed the chocolate before plundering her mouth. He tasted of wine and chocolate and kissed like her like he had every right to.

To prove him wrong, she kissed him back. Two could play this sexual domination game. Her hand slid into his hair. The other found its way under his shirt to explore his back. Damn, he felt good. All hard muscles. Strong. Safe.

His lips left hers and trailed kisses over to her ear where he whispered, "*Dieu*, Maya, you're driving me insane." His breath was hot against her skin, scorching a path followed by his lips. As he traced the cord of her neck with his tongue, she felt her bra give way. His hand eased between their bodies to cup her breast. She moaned in pleasure as his thumb circled her already-hard nipple. His other hand slid into the back pocket of her shorts and pulled her against him so she could feel his erection. She shimmied her hips against him, and his whole body shuddered in response.

They'd gone from negotiating a truce to removing her clothes in seconds. It wasn't just a loss of control, it was a total annihilation of restraint. Despite her reputation, she wasn't one to jump in bed with someone within hours of meeting them. But it was like she'd known Jacques a lot longer. Or been waiting for him. That idea was enough of a shock to snap her back to reality.

"Wait, Jacques. Do you have protection?"

He stopped instantly and stepped back, his breathing as rapid and shallow as hers. His hair was thoroughly disheveled, his shirt was half-unbuttoned—when had she done that?—and an impressive bulge distorted the front of his pants. He was so sexy … why had she stopped? *Oh, yeah, because we only freaking met yesterday.*

His eyes were dazed. "I only meant to kiss the chocolate away. I didn't mean to…" He waved his hand in the air in a Gallic gesture for *how the hell did this happen?*

She refastened her bra and tried to reengage her brain. "You don't have to apologize. If I hadn't wanted you to kiss me, you'd be lying on the ground clutching your manhood. This was inevitable. I think we both need to work on our restraint. Especially now that we know it's too…" What word did you use to describe all-out, mind-blowing pleasure?

"Explosive?"

"I'll go with that. So maybe we need a couple of rules."

"You don't seem like a rules type of woman."

"I'm not. But I'm trying to turn over a new forest, remember?"

"New forest?"

"More than a leaf. I want to start a new life. I can't do that wrapped around you. So, rule one: Hands off, and that applies to both of us. Rule two: Bring a condom for when rule one fails." She was nothing if not realistic. He was right; she'd never been good with restrictions, even her own.

"Agreed." He handed her the keys to the vehicle. "Why don't you get in and turn on the air conditioner? I need a moment before I can sit." He wandered back down to the lake.

She climbed into the SUV, started the engine, and cranked the AC to high, directing the flow at her face.

She'd just gotten her breathing under control when her cell phone rang. Only one person had this number: her brother. And he knew it was for emergencies only.

Sean didn't even bother with pleasantries. "Maya, the RCMP were just at my door."

"Is it Dad? Mom?" Her heart stalled then went into overdrive.

"They're fine. The police were asking about you."

Shit, shit, shit. The cops had found Sean. The trouble she was in now was monumental compared to the trifle she'd left behind as a teen. Hopefully Big Tony wouldn't think to check if she'd ever changed her name. Maya Murphy had only ever existed in British Columbia. She'd become a Tessier before she'd arrived in Montreal, and as far as she knew, Tony Chartrand's criminal organization was limited to the east side of the country.

"What did the police say?" She held her breath.

"They want to know where you are. They've issued a subpoena for you to testify in court."

"I can't come back. If I testify, I'll be dead in days."

"They say they can protect you." Her brother had

always been on the good side of the law. He still believed their promises.

"Like they protected the other two witnesses? Did they tell you they were dead, which is why they now want me to testify?"

"God, Maya. What have you gotten yourself involved with?"

"I was just in the wrong place at the wrong time with the wrong people. You didn't tell them where I was, did you?"

"No, of course not. Because I don't know where you are. You only gave me this phone number. And before you panic, I'm calling from a burner phone. I have learned a few things from the kids I coach. And give the cops some credit. They kept it very quiet that they figured out we were related. I just want to give you the heads-up that they're looking for you. Be careful, sis. I love you."

"I love you, too, Sean."

She ended the call and put the phone back in her bag. Her hand shook as she ran it over her mouth. A mouth that minutes ago had been ravaged by the man still standing at the lake. At least she was keeping up her record of epic mistakes.

Would she even get a chance to turn over a new forest—before it was burned down?

Chapter 6

Jacques swirled the amber liquid in his glass. He was drinking cognac, which was stupid because it reminded him of Maya's eyes. But since almost everything he encountered reminded him of some part of Maya, it really didn't matter. After the kiss at the lake, he'd needed time and distance to rethink his strategy.

He was a strong man, but he knew his limits. And evidently the line was drawn at a hot redhead living a hundred meters from his bedroom. So he'd gone back to Paris to confer with his lawyers and had asked Daniel to take Grand-Papa on a mini-holiday to keep him out of Maya's clutches.

But here Jacques was, back at the chateau, because Daniel had returned to work and someone needed to keep an eye on Grand-Papa. And Maya. They may have had a truce, but that didn't mean he couldn't plan his attack for when the armistice ended.

He had a bill to present to her, detailing all the costs incurred in maintaining the cottage and vines for the past seven decades. He'd delved into her finances, and she didn't have anywhere near enough to pay it. He'd force her to sell the land, but let her stay on in the cottage to appease his grandfather—and the stupid, irresponsible part of him that enjoyed her company, her feistiness, and the way she didn't give a damn about his wealth or power.

He slung back the last of his drink and was about

to finish getting undressed for bed when a scream shattered the quiet night. A woman's scream. He raced out of his room and down the stairs before he even thought to grab his phone in case he needed to call the police. But he wasn't about to go back upstairs for it. He'd use Maya's if it came to that.

So as not to alert any intruder, he ran along the grass, hurdling the small box hedges that were meticulously cut into fancy patterns. He misjudged one and went sprawling into a bed of flowers. The sound of a shovel hitting gravel reached his ears. Was Maya defending herself from an assault? Forget stealth. He pushed himself up and covered the rest of the distance as fast as he could. Three meters from Maya he skidded to a halt.

She was digging. With a shovel. At midnight. He was about to ask what she was doing when a dog raced up to him, teeth bared.

Maya whirled around, her mouth opening in surprise when she saw him. "Princess, heel!" The dog gave one last growl before retreating to Maya's side, never taking its eyes off Jacques.

"Maya, what are you doing?"

"I'm digging a moat."

"A moat?" He'd had a couple of drinks, but Maya must have had more. He needed to take the shovel from her before she hurt herself. He stepped closer, but the dog growled again.

"Yes, all the great houses have them. So I thought the cottage should as well. I can't decide whether to fill it with alligators or sharks once I get it dug."

She pushed a strand of hair behind her ear as she

leaned on her shovel. A dead rat lay a few feet away. She was obviously about to bury it. But she was in a flirtatious mood, so much more relaxed than she'd been at the end of their day on Saturday, so he played along.

"How will you stop the alligators from crawling out? And I think sharks require salt water," he said.

"True. What do you suggest?"

"Piranhas."

"Excellent choice. Piranhas, it is. Why doesn't the chateau have a moat?" The deep V of her dress barely restrained her full breasts as she lifted the next shovelful of dirt. He forced his brain to answer her question. His body was doing its own thing.

"It had a moat until the eighteenth century. Then it was filled in, as the water stank and bred mosquitoes. It was worse for the people stuck inside than for invaders. If you walk around the perimeter of the property, you can still see where it was located."

"I forgot about mosquitoes. I hate them. Guess I'll have to find another way to keep out the bad guys."

"Your dog seems be doing that job." The name Princess must have been ironic, because it was the ugliest dog he'd ever seen. If you chose the worst bits of each breed and put them into one animal, you'd get Princess.

"Princess is a great dog, aren't you, gorgeous?" Maya bent and scratched the dog on the head and was rewarded with a canine look of love. "I rescued her from animal control. Can you believe someone abandoned her at the side of the road? She's an excellent guard dog. I didn't know, however, that she also took on rats. Come meet her." She grabbed Princess's collar and motioned Jacques towards her. Although the dog growled, it wasn't as menacing as before. When he stood only a foot away, Maya stepped forward, put a hand on his shoulder, and kissed his cheek. "There. Now she knows you're a friend." The dog began to wag its tail seconds before it stuck its nose in his privates, which were clocking an evident interest in Maya. Jacques's breath whooshed out audibly.

"Sorry, she's a bit enthusiastic. Can I offer you a drink for coming to my rescue? I take it you heard me scream."

"Yes, to both. Are you okay?" He searched her face and body for sign of injury.

"I'm fine. Princess caught a rat and dropped it in my lap. I didn't think you'd be able to hear me in the big house. Or were you out for a walk?" This time it was her eyes that searched his body. He looked down as well; aside from the rather evident tenting in the front of his pants, his shirt was mostly unbuttoned and he had grass stains on his knees.

"I was in the house about to go to bed. But the glass is thin and the French Heritage Society won't let us replace it. Sound travels rather well."

"I'll have to remember to keep quiet, then. And I appreciate your efforts to make me feel less disheveled." She pulled a flower petal out of his hair. "Just let me finish digging this rat grave, and then I'll get you a drink."

"How about I bury the rat? You're not really dressed for digging."

Her light tinkle of laughter didn't help the

situation. "I'll be on the back terrace when you're done."

***

Maya turned at Jacques's approach. Somehow she'd expected him to come through the house, not around it. He stood on the edge of the terrace, but she couldn't tell if he was amazed or horrified. Maybe she'd overdone it a bit with the candles. But for a city girl, the country was too damn dark. And it was way too hot inside to sleep, or do anything else for that matter. So she'd lit every candle she could find and set up a little oasis in the backyard. Until Princess had brought her unwelcome gift, that is.

"Are you expecting someone?"

She glanced around. It did look like a scene out of a seduction. "You never know who may turn up." Rising from the lounger, she grabbed the bottle of wine and two glasses she'd left on the kitchen counter. "Your granddad brought over some wine. It looks pretty expensive, so I was saving it for a special occasion. I guess you'll do."

Jacques took the wine from her hand and examined the label in the flickering candlelight. Standing close, she could smell his spicy aftershave and licked her lips. His eyes followed the movement of her tongue.

"It's from our vineyard, one of our best years. However, the value in wine is enjoying the moment when it's consumed. It's just a beverage; it's the people you drink it with that are the real treasure."

She swallowed. "I hope you don't do your own

marketing. You'll never get top dollar for your product with that slogan."

"I employ a company to market the wines. But it's the truth. You can have the most expensive wine in the world, but if you drink it alone or with people you don't particularly like, it's worthless."

"Do you think I'm worth it?" She put her hands on her hip and dared him to deny it.

"Of course you are." He didn't even hesitate. Smart man. "Would you like me to teach you to properly taste wine?" He uncorked the bottle with ease and poured two glasses. Just an inch. Maybe he didn't think she was worth the whole bottle.

"Why, so you can turn me into a wine snob?"

"I would never want you to be anything other than what you are now."

What the hell was that supposed to mean? She took the glass he offered her. "So, you think I'm perfect just the way I am?"

His gaze locked on hers. "With the small exception of not knowing how to truly appreciate a fine wine."

"All right, Mr. Vintner, show me how to"—she put on her snobbiest accent—"truly appreciate a fine wine."

"It would be my pleasure."

Damn it, why did he have to keep using that word? With the huskiness of his voice and the way his eyes caressed her, she was already wobbly, and she hadn't even had a drink yet. What was with that? This wasn't her first rodeo. She'd been attracted to men before. Hell, she hadn't been a virgin since her sixteenth birthday. But none of the men she'd been with had ever made her feel so … so … melty. It was damned annoying.

He led her over to the lounger with a hand at her back then sat next to her, their thighs centimeters apart.

Wine tasting—it had seemed such a good idea at the time.

"First step is to analyze the color." His voice dropped, making the moment more intimate than it should have been. They were talking liquid, not lingerie. But the passion she'd seen in him at the winery was back. He'd told her about several of his companies, but it was only the vineyard that seemed to excite him. Wine flowed in Jacques's veins. "It's a little hard to tell in this light, but what do you see?"

She held her glass up to the nearest candle, swirling it as he did. "It's maroon with hints of sienna," she said.

"Good color comparison. Your artistic talent is showing. Next, smell the wine deeply and pick out two scents. Take your time. They can be hard to identify at first, but the more you do this, the more aromas you can smell."

It took three deep inhalations before she could concentrate on the scent of the wine instead of the scent of Jacques. "Pepper … and … raspberries?"

"Excellent. You are a wine snob in the making. Smell again. Can you pick up the vanilla?"

She stuck her tongue out at him but then sniffed the wine again. "Yes, just a hint. Do you actually add vanilla?"

"No, it comes from the oak barrels where the wine is aged. Now taste the wine. Take a large sip to coat your mouth, then a few small sips to identify the flavors."

She did as he suggested, rolling the wine around in her mouth. She closed her eyes to concentrate. When she opened them again, Jacques was staring at her.

"Am I doing something wrong?"

"No, you're doing everything perfectly. I've just never seen a person concentrate so hard on tasting wine. It's adorable."

God, she hadn't been called adorable since she was six. "I want to get it right."

"There is no right or wrong. It's what you taste—your palate."

"You mean at last there's something I can't fail at?" She took another sip, the different flavors of the wine revealing themselves in stages.

"Is it sweet or dry?" Jacques prompted.

"Dry."

"Did the wine start bold and finish subtle, or did the intensity build as you tasted it?"

"Um, the intensity built?" They were still talking about wine, right?

"Yes. Or so the experts say."

"That's it?"

Banked desire flared in his eyes. "Well, there is my favorite way to taste wine. But it involves breaking rule number one."

"I wouldn't want a silly rule to hinder my education. What is your favorite way to taste wine, Jacques?"

He placed both their glasses on the ground beside the chair then threaded a hand through her hair and drew her face closer to his. "On the lips of someone who's just savored it."

"Is this what people do at all those fancy wine-tasting events?"

"No, this is for private lessons only."

"Private lessons are the best," she said. Her eyes drifted closed as his mouth touched hers. At first his tongue just traced the outline of her lips. But as she parted them, he slipped inside. The kiss was gentle, explorative, but she wanted more. Needed more. One of her hands slid into his hair, and the silkiness of the strands slipped between her fingers. At her response, he angled her head to gain greater access. His lips challenged, teased, and tempted until she was kissing him as thoroughly as he was her. Their hands joined the party, and it wasn't until a breeze drifted over her naked chest that she realized he'd slid the dress from her shoulders and bared her from the waist up. She lay back on the lounger, drawing him with her.

He cupped her breast, his thumb teasing her nipple in a silent torment. She arched into his hand, aching for more. Jacques's lips finally left hers, trailing fiery kisses down her neck until he took one hard nipple in his mouth and flicked it with his tongue before sucking it gently. A shocked cry of pleasure escaped her mouth and he released her, raising his head to stare into her eyes. *Now that was rising intensity.*

"You are a dangerous woman, Maya Tessier. More intoxicating than the most potent wine. One taste is never enough. When I touch you, all reason goes out of my head, and I become that wild man you wanted to see. I don't like it." He readjusted her dress, covering her breasts, then stood. Picking up his wineglass, he moved to the edge of the patio, his back to her.

She hauled in a deep breath. It was one thing to play with fire, but this explosive chemistry had the potential to burn them both. It was time to permanently douse the flames of this out-of-control lust. "I am dangerous, Jacques. More than you know. Men who love me end up dead or in prison. I don't want that to happen to you."

He turned then, but it was too dark to read his expression. She slung back the wine, not bothering to taste it. Liquid courage was all she had to tell him her story.

"What do you mean?" He refilled her glass. And his own. Then he sat on the chair next to the table. Candlelight flickered over the hard planes of his face.

"My first boyfriend was a drug dealer and a gang member. I pretended I didn't know for a while, but when he gave me diamond earrings worth two grand for my sixteenth birthday, I figured the money wasn't from his paper route."

"What happened to him?" His tone was neutral, as though he were asking about her day. Apparently it was no biggie that she'd just confessed to consorting with a criminal.

"He was on his way to pick me up for my high school graduation party. First he collected my best friend. Then, two blocks from my place, he and Kelsey were shot to death. I remember being mad that he was late, then hearing the sirens. I thought maybe he'd been arrested. My brother went to check it out and told me the news. If I'd been picked up first, I'd be dead, not Kelsey."

"Is that why you went to live with your great-grandmother?"

"Yes. My parents wanted me out of that life, away from my former friends, so they sent me to Gran-Gran. I even changed my last name to distance myself from my past. She took me in on two conditions."

"What were they?"

"One, that I stop swearing. She hated profanity. Two, that I keep away from gangs and drug dealers. Unfortunately, I only kept one of those conditions."

"You stopped swearing?"

"Yeah. I was good for a few years. Gran-Gran and I got on great. She loved art and encouraged me in my studies, pulling some strings to get my paintings into a gallery run by one of her friends."

"And then?"

"I got impatient. I wanted instant success. Raj, my first boyfriend, had showered me with money and gifts. I hated having to scrape every last penny together to make my bus fare to go to class. Then I met this guy."

Jacques shifted in his seat. He was no longer looking at her. Good, she'd turned him off. It was better this way. Let him know how bad she truly was. Then he'd leave her in peace and she could get on with her art. It was what Gran-Gran had wanted. It was what she should have done in the first place.

"He was a criminal, too?"

"Victor was a lot more discreet than my first boyfriend. I should have read the signs, but I was too stupid. For one, a computer sales rep shouldn't have had the money he did. But he told me it was family money. And he was so nice. He bought me things, treated me to dinner in fancy restaurants, drove a cool car, took me to clubs. Then one night we were at a house party, some other guy grabbed me, and a fight broke out. Victor stabbed the guy in the heart and he died. At the trial I learned they were both drug dealers and had a history going way back. Evidently Victor had uttered death threats against this guy before. So the court found him guilty of first-degree murder, and he's serving a life sentence."

"You don't do things by half, do you?" He put his wineglass on the small table, and she was sure he was about to walk away. "Do you use drugs?"

"I've tried a few, but I don't like the way they make me feel. I get sick, not high. So I haven't touched them in years. And I stopped smoking when Gran-Gran started having trouble breathing after a bout of pneumonia."

"Anything else?"

"No." She hadn't told him about Etienne, or that Big Tony wanted her dead. But there was only so much soul-baring a woman could do in one night.

Jacques picked up his wine and took a drink. Was he trying to get the taste of her out of his mouth? Eventually, he spoke. "I'm not a criminal. I'm not a drug-dealer. And as enticing as you are, I'm pretty sure you won't turn me into one. But I appreciate your honesty, so I'll reciprocate. I married to secure an heir. I was busy working, turning around companies my father looted to fund his playboy lifestyle. I didn't have time to date, and I didn't want a woman to distract me from business. So I took my mother's suggestion and married her best friend's daughter. Clarisse was beautiful, poised, and so completely self-centered that she never noticed if I was around or not. There was no love between us, but we got on tolerably. The first spark of happiness in our marriage was when she told me she was pregnant. Then she killed our child with her recklessness."

"At last, something we have in common. We both make lousy choices when it comes to our personal lives."

"Well, I'm never going to put myself in a position again where a woman has the power to destroy my world. Not only do you make me lose control, but you seem to attract trouble, and I don't need that in my life."

"I understand."

"Then I wish you a good night." He rose, and after a slight inclination of his head in her direction, disappeared around the side of the cottage.

If Jacques knew her life was in danger, he'd probably find a way to bar her from her only safe refuge. She'd have to keep her distance and her head down.

So what if her heart ached like she'd just lost something important?

Chapter 7

Jacques woke with a pounding headache. He rolled over, but the empty sheets taunted him. Even when he was married, Clarisse had always insisted on having her own room. So why did his bed seem so empty now?

A faint buzzing sound infiltrated his brain. Either a swarm of bees had invaded his bedroom or a gardener was on a drunken rampage with a hedge trimmer. Either way, Jacques wasn't going back to sleep. He flopped out of bed and peeked behind the curtain to see if the topiary unicorn stallions were now all geldings. But aside from horrifically blinding sunlight, the garden was clear of crazed staff. The sound appeared to be coming from the cottage.

What was the woman up to now? Maybe if he brought her coffee and pastries again she'd shut the hell up. He could also deliver the maintenance invoice and sort out the land issue before the grape harvest.

By the time he parked his grandfather's electric golf cart in front of the cottage, the noise was deafening. There was no point knocking; she'd never hear him. He ventured around the side of the building carefully, in case he startled Princess and ended up being gelded himself. The dog was nowhere to be seen. But Maya was up a ladder, clad in coveralls, armed with a hard hat, face protector, and thick gloves, and wielding a big-ass chainsaw. Another chunk of the huge log fell to the ground. She leaned back, her head cocked to one side as if considering her next cut, and wobbled on the ladder. He raced over to stabilize it before she had a nasty accident.

She shut off the chainsaw, but his ears still buzzed with the noise. When she raised the face shield, her smile blinded him almost as much as the sun had earlier.

"I'm going to get you a cape."

Every time he talked with her, he felt like he'd walked into the middle of the conversation. "A cape?"

"Yeah. You're always rescuing me. You need a cape. Any hope I could convince you to show up in Lycra next time?"

"Not a chance."

"Pity. You've got an ass that could really rock the Spandex."

"Thanks … I think. Can I ask what you're doing? And don't you dare say—"

"Building a catapult?"

"*Dieu*, woman. Why is it so hard to get a straight answer out of you?" She was still several rungs up the ladder, and his head felt like it was about to fall off, which in his current state would be a blessed mercy.

"Because you ask too-obvious questions. I can't help teasing."

"Can you tease at ground level? I've got a killer headache, and staring up at you is making it worse."

She climbed down, carefully placing the guard on the chainsaw. "I rather liked having the height advantage. But you do look like you've just had the shit scared out of you, so I'll be nice for once."

"I have coffee and pastries if you promise not to use the chainsaw again until I feel better."

"Deal. I need to map out the rest of my cuts anyway."

She pulled off the hard hat and shook her hair loose. The auburn strands caught the light, and it was like his own private sunset. When she started to unzip the coveralls, he made a strategic retreat to get the promised breakfast. He was in no state to deal with a disrobing Maya.

How the hell had he missed the massive log in her backyard yesterday? Probably because it had been dark, and because he'd been concentrating too much on her.

By the time he entered her kitchen through the open back door, she'd set the small table. Her hair was piled on top of her head in a messy bun, the tattoo at the base of her neck calling out to be explored by his lips.

She motioned for him to sit. "Sorry if I woke you," she said as she poured coffee for them both. "The wood was delivered yesterday and I'm dying to get carving. But it's been so hot that I figured I'd better start early; I have to wear all that gear…" Her voice turned into a buzz and he found it difficult to focus on her face. What was she saying? "Jacques?"

"Sorry, I…" He closed his eyes, willing the hammering at his temples to stop just long enough for him to get back to bed.

"You really are sick. Should I call a doctor or get your grandfather?"

"No. It's just a migraine. If you could drive me back to the house… I brought my grandfather's cart, but I don't think I can see well enough to make it home."

"I don't think you'll make it to the cart. Come with me." He was too busy keeping his head on his neck to argue. She put an arm around his waist and led him up the stairs to her room. "Sit." She left his side for a second and the room went blissfully dark. Still, he closed his eyes as the room started to spin. He opened them again when he felt her fingers against his throat.

"Maya…"

"Relax, I'm not about to ravage you. Can you undress yourself? My mother suffered from migraines, and I've got some stuff that will help. Unless you have a prescription at the big house that I can get for you."

"No prescription. Don't get them often enough." He forced his fingers to work the buttons on his shirt. She was gone an eternity, but he still hadn't got his belt undone before she was standing in front of him again.

"Here, let me," she said. She pushed his hands away and made quick work of his belt and the zipper on his jeans. A groan escaped his throat. In every scenario where he'd imagined Maya removing his clothes, he hadn't been struggling to remain conscious. "Lay down now with your head at the foot of the bed."

He did as she instructed, unable to ask why he shouldn't lay down the proper way. Being horizontal felt too good to question the orientation. She propped his feet up and wrapped them in a warm towel before gently pulling a light sheet over him. She then put his hands on something cool. He closed his eyes, relief already stemming from her care.

"Do you mind being touched when you're like this? I used to give my mother cranial massages to help her get to sleep."

"Go ahead. I'll let you know if..." Her fingers put light, then firmer, pressure on his temples, and a strong smell of peppermint and lavender filled the air.

Dieu, Maya's touch was magic.

***

He was in hell. It was the only way to account for being so hot. At least his head felt better, which seemed odd given his damnation. He opened his eyes to check out his new residence. Hell dressed as heaven—ingenious. Had he known demons looked like Maya, he wouldn't have worried so much about his eventual destination.

Maybe it was heaven after all. Maya certainly looked at peace. She was curled up on the bed, her head resting on the pillow next to his feet. He shifted to give her more room, and her eyes fluttered open. *Merde*, he'd gone from migraine to heart attack. Although he could think of worse places to die than Maya's bed. Too bad it hadn't been after an epic round of lovemaking.

"Hi." Her voice was so soft that he knew she'd spoken only because her lips had moved.

"Hi. How long have I slept?"

"Five hours, give or take."

"I'm sorry. You probably had plans for the day."

"Nothing that couldn't be rescheduled."

He eased himself into an upright position. So far, so good. The headache was gone, and the dizziness faded after a few seconds. But where were his clothes?

"I'll get some lunch together while you dress. I put a fresh towel out if you want a shower first." Maya rose regally to her feet, picked up the book that had fallen on the floor, and left the room without looking back.

The lure of a cool shower was too much to resist, so fifteen minutes later he joined her in the kitchen. He scrubbed his hand along his stubble-covered jaw as he contemplated his hostess bustling about the kitchen, putting together a fruit salad. She sliced with efficient movements, but her hips swayed to a different tune.

Princess saw him before Maya did. The dog gave him a wary eye before coming over to inspect him. Maya turned when the dog gave a low *woof* in greeting.

"Feel better now?" she asked, handing him a glass of water. How had she known he was thirsty? He hadn't been so cosseted since he was a child struck down with chicken pox. But back then a fifty-something nanny had cared for him, not a gorgeous twenty-something femme fatale.

"Much. Unfortunately, large portions of this morning are a complete blur. Without wanting to be rude, how did I wind up upside down in your bed wearing only my underwear?"

"You don't remember the trapeze swing at all?" For a millisecond he searched his brain before he saw the teasing light in Maya's eyes. "Evidently you had some weird objection to me using a chainsaw at five o'clock in the morning. You lured me away from my work with pastries, but then seemed on the point of passing out. So I took you upstairs, made you comfortable, and you fell asleep. Your virtue is intact, no need to worry."

"I wasn't worried. Just wouldn't want to have missed anything."

"Nothing worth writing in the diary." She shrugged and went back to slicing an apple. "I've got yogurt and fruit salad and, of course, the pastries you brought with you this morning. After a migraine my mother said her stomach could only handle simple foods. But if you want something more substantial…"

"No, what you have is perfect. Again, I'm sorry. I haven't had an episode like that…" *Since Clarisse died.* "…in a long time."

"I can't bear to see anyone in pain. I did what I could to help."

Help was an understatement. Last time he'd had a migraine, he'd been in bed for two days with it. Maya was a miracle worker.

He grabbed a piece of apple from her pile. Not much had changed in the small kitchen in the ten days since she'd moved in, except that now it looked lived in. Loved. A jug of fresh flowers graced the table, a few herbs grew in pots on the windowsill, and a painting smock hung on a peg by the door to the small anteroom. Through the open door he spotted an easel, and he made his way over to see what she'd painted. On a large canvas was an extremely good painting of Daniel in his racing overalls, his helmet

70

tucked under his arm.

So, Maya had chosen to paint his younger brother. Granted, she had asked Jacques first and he'd refused. He couldn't blame her for moving on to Daniel. But maybe he'd misread the passion between them. Maybe she preferred his brother after all.

"What do you think?" Her sultry, sexy voice washed over him. He should skip lunch and go back to the house.

"It's very good. Are you waiting for Daniel to come back to complete his face?"

"No, it's done. He gave me a couple of publicity photos."

"Then why is it blurry?" Jacques stepped closer. Every sponsor badge, every tiny design on Daniel's crash helmet was in clear perspective.

"Daniel the racer knows exactly who he is; that's why his racing gear is clear. Daniel the man is not so sure. So I've only drawn his features in lightly. Until he figures out who he is—beyond his career—this is how I will see him."

"Really?" Jacques studied the painting some more. How had Maya seen so perfectly behind the facade Daniel showed to the world? As far as Jacques knew, only he and his grandfather were aware of the turmoil that drove his younger brother to live life on the edge and keep others at arm's length.

"Yes. He pretends to be a playboy, but I think it's a front, something he feigns to keep people from actually knowing him." She was spot on. Jacques shifted his weight from one foot to the other.

"And how do you view me?"

"Would you like to see?"

Did he really want to know what this woman thought of him? Talk about shining a light on a dark place. "You've painted me as well?"

"Not yet. I sketched you while you slept. I'm sorry if you consider it an invasion of privacy. But you were in my bed." Maya left and returned a few seconds later with the book she'd taken from the bedroom. It was a sketchpad. She flipped a few pages, stared at one for a moment, then handed the pad to him.

He sucked in a deep breath. *Mon Dieu.*

Chapter 8

Maya stared at Jacques's face as he examined her
sketch. While he'd slept, she'd become obsessed with
the beauty of his features, relaxed of all the worries
and responsibilities he carried around with him. That
wasn't what concerned her, however. It was the look
she'd put in his eyes. A look of love, of longing, of
hope. That was how she wanted him to be. Not the
bitter, resigned man who stood in her cottage, holding
one of her best pieces of art in his hands.

"You've sketched me with my eyes open."

"Yes, I propped them open with toothpicks. You
were so gone you didn't notice." She tried for a tease,
but he wasn't having it this time. He waited. The only
sound was Princess panting in the other room.

"Why have you drawn me like this?"

"Because that's the man you could be. If you
could just let go of the past."

His gaze met hers and she read the warning loud
and clear before he even spoke. "I can never be this
man, Maya. If this is who you're waiting for, I'm
sorry to disappoint you. My past made me who I am
today. It can't be undone."

She opened her mouth to refute the statement but
closed it again. You could lead a man to a mirror, but
you couldn't make him see. "Let me tell you what
I've learned about the past. If you don't come to
terms with it, it will destroy your future. Do you
know how many mornings I woke up over the past

ten years wishing I'd made different choices in my life? Every single one of them. If I hadn't gotten involved with Raj or any of the others; if I'd studied harder in school, gone to university, got a degree, got a regular job… Know what? I didn't. I've had to become who I am today to survive. But I'm determined not to stay that way. I'm going to move on with my life. Make myself better. Do something worthy. Make up for my past mistakes. I promised Gran-Gran I would, and I won't let her down. You have a choice, too. You can continue to live your life in fear of more heartache. Or you can move on. It's entirely up to you. My advice? Don't rule happiness out of your future. Don't let Clarisse kill you, too."

He stared at her as if she'd just slapped him. Nothing like hitting a man recovering from a debilitating migraine over the head with some hard truths. A strategic retreat was needed.

"Let's eat," she said. She turned on her heel and strode back into the kitchen, fussing with the salad until she was back in control.

When he sat down, however, it wasn't her emotions she was worried about revealing. A trickle of sweat dripped into the pool that had formed in her bra. There was only so much moisture Victoria could keep secret.

"It's like an oven in here. You haven't got the heating on by mistake, have you?" he asked.

"No, of course not. But the whole front of the house, including my bedroom, is south facing. And the frothy white curtains don't keep out the heat. So by midday it gets warm."

"It's unbearable. How have you slept?"

"Mostly on the sofa. In the evening I open all the windows and doors, hoping to catch a cross breeze. By midnight it's usually cool enough to sleep downstairs. At least it's cured me of sleeping in all morning—although for some bizarre reason, my neighbor objects to me firing up a chain saw at 5:00 a.m."

Jacques opened his mouth, but it was his grandfather's voice she heard. "There you are. I've been looking for you all morning, Jacques. I guess next time I should try the cottage first." Charles appeared at the back door and tipped his hat in greeting.

As though he were caught somewhere he shouldn't be, Jacques jumped to his feet. "I came to stop the racket Maya was making and had to wait out a migraine," he replied.

"Okay, if that's the story you're going for." Charles chuckled, his blue eyes full of laughter.

That sounded to Maya like an opening for an argument. "Would you like to join us, Charles? We're having a late breakfast, or is it an early lunch?" She rose to grab another place setting, but in doing so, wound up centimeters from Jacques. Now she and Jacques looked even guiltier.

"No, thank you. I've already eaten. I just came to reclaim my golf cart." He took his hat off and waved it in front of his face. "*Mon Dieu*, it's hot in here. I forgot this place doesn't have air conditioning. I'm so sorry, Maya."

"It's okay. I spend most of my time outside anyway," she replied.

"Nonsense," Charles said. "Until the heat breaks,

75

you can stay up at the chateau. We have air conditioning, at least in the bedrooms." Jacques did not look pleased at his grandfather's suggestion.

"The Heritage Society won't let you put in better windows, but you've got air conditioning?"

"We didn't ask," Jacques answered. "Most of the bedrooms have secret passages to them. Evidently when the house was constructed, my ancestors liked to have discreet access to their mistresses' bedchambers. We simply routed the air conditioning ducts through these spaces."

"Clever. And is that all the passages are used for these days—air conditioning? There's not a flurry of bed swapping every night?"

"With me, Daniel, and Grand-Papa the only residents? No way." Jacques moved towards his grandfather, who was still looking at her expectantly.

Her resistance wasn't strong enough yet to sleep in the same building as Jacques.

"Thanks for the offer, but I'm fine here."

Charles wasn't even subtle when he nudged Jacques. Maya hid a smile by pretending to drink her iced coffee. Big, important Jacques de Launay controlled by his elderly grandparent.

"You are most welcome to stay at the chateau, Maya. In fact, I insist," Jacques said.

"Is this your plan to prevent me from starting up the chainsaw again at the crack of dawn?"

"Of course not. Your comfort is my only consideration." But not even he could say that lie with a straight face.

Looked like she was moving to the big house. Into the lair of the beast.

***

Damn Grand-Papa and his meddling. Now he had temptation under his roof. Worse, his grandfather had insisted Clarisse's old room was the only one suitable for their guest. Forty-two bedrooms, and Maya was to have the one connected to Jacques's.

But arguing with his grandfather was about as useful as complaining to a rock about its shape. Jacques led Maya up the stairs and to the far end of a long corridor. He halted two doors from the end and sucked in a deep breath.

He opened the door and gestured for her to enter. Maybe she'd be so disgusted by the decor, she'd insist on another room—or return to the cottage. Almost everything was in shades of pink, and there were ruffles on the bedspread. Ruffles. It looked like Barbie had thrown up. But at least it was cool. He wouldn't have asked his worst enemy to sleep in the cottage in such heat. And as much as it galled him to admit it, Maya was no enemy. Inconvenient, unconventional, irrational, and possibly dangerous to his self-control, yes. But he'd bet money she never set out to hurt anyone deliberately.

He placed her bag on the bench at the end of the bed. "There's a closet through that door if you want to hang up anything. Or I can ask one of the staff to do it for you."

"I'm pretty sure I can manage to hang up the few things I've brought. What's through that door?" She pointed to another panel at the opposite side of the room, near the bed.

He strode over and opened it. "Washroom. I'll

get some towels for you." He pulled out his phone and called the housekeeper, Marie, as Maya wandered around the room.

"My bedroom is through the connecting door in the washroom," he said after returning his phone to his pocket.

"Wait, what? You've put me in a room that connects to yours?" Maya's arms were crossed under her breasts, thrusting them up, but he forced his eyes to remain on her face.

"Is that a problem? There's a lock on the door if you're worried. Or you can choose one of the other rooms, and I'll ask the housekeeper to get it ready. Grand-Papa is downstairs. Daniel's room is down at the other end of the hall, but he's away at the moment, doing a photo shoot for some sponsor, I think." He turned away as he mentioned his younger brother so she couldn't see his expression.

"Do you think I want to be closer to Daniel?"

"Most women do." He shrugged.

She strode over to him and put her hand on his cheek, waiting until his gaze met hers. *Dieu*, did she have to touch him all the time? It was … addictive. "I am not most women. Yes, your brother is good-looking and charming, but there is no attraction between us. Now, your grandfather on the other hand, that sparkle in his eyes…"

Jacques laughed. She never said what he expected.

"Speaking of my grandfather, please be careful with him. He's had his heart broken several times. Don't play with his affections."

She dropped her hand from his cheek and looked

upset that he'd even suggest such a thing. "I wouldn't. Gran-Gran used to talk of him so much, I kind of feel like he's my grandfather, too. I will be as protective of him as you are."

He searched her eyes. She was such a mixture, all bad-girl biker chick one minute, softhearted migraine-reliever the next. But she seemed genuine, and, at the moment, all he could see was honest caring. Either she was a masterful player or had hidden depths. With a blind leap of faith, he replied, "Okay. I'll see you later, then. I have work to do. I should be recovered enough to see my computer screen now."

"Don't overdo it, Jacques. It's better to take a day off than lose a whole week. Why don't you come with Charles and me? Yesterday when he dropped off the wine he talked about a rose he and Gran-Gran had planted. He's going to show it to me today. Plus, you'll be able to make sure I don't wheedle any more of your inheritance out of him."

And vixen Maya was back. "There's nothing left to take. He transferred it all to me years ago."

"See, you have nothing to worry about." She grabbed a big, floppy, white hat and strode towards the door. "We'll be in the rose garden if your paranoia kicks up again." Before she left, she turned back and blew him a kiss.

He twirled his wedding ring on his finger in the middle of his late wife's god-awful pink bedroom. He'd kept the ring on to remind himself not to put his happiness in the hands of another woman again. Except Maya was right: he was giving Clarisse power over his future. He had to rely on his judgment not to make the same mistake again. Judgment that was seriously compromised by Maya's nearness.

The maintenance invoice still sat on his desk. He'd forgotten to take it earlier in his haste to stop Maya making so much noise. He could give it to her now, force her to sell the land to him, and completely destroy this chain of attraction that got stronger every time he was with her. But given the care she'd shown him this morning and the obvious bond of affection between her and his grandfather, it seemed churlish. He pulled off his wedding band and put it in his pocket.

He'd wait and see what happened. The land wasn't going anywhere.

Chapter 9

"You know Jacques is not going to like this," Maya said, but she handed the helmet to Charles anyway.

His blue eyes twinkled. "What Jacques doesn't know won't hurt him."

She fastened the strap under Charles's chin and then helped him mount her motorbike. They'd spent every morning together for the past two weeks, exploring the gardens or rooms in the chateau. Charles kept her amused with stories of past inhabitants, including the ancestor who had eight mistresses at one time and got so lost in the secret passages, he went missing for two days until finally emerging in his wife's bedchamber. His neglected wife had been so incensed at her husband's philandering that she kept him tied to her bed until she was sure she was pregnant. After that, he'd dismissed his mistresses and never slept with anyone other than his wife again.

Was Charles hinting that she should tie Jacques to her bed until he got her pregnant? (Not that she hadn't considered it once or twice, minus the pregnancy part.) Every night they sat next to each other at the dinner table, trying to ignore the chemistry between them. Their truce was lasting so far, and Jacques seemed determined to keep his hands off her. She should have been happy.

She wasn't.

To mask her frustrated groan, she flicked the

Ducati's engine to life. "I don't think your grandson would agree with you," she shouted over her shoulder. Charles's arms came around her waist, and she slowly drove them to the front gates and back to the chateau, Princess running beside them.

She hadn't been off the grounds since she'd moved up to the big house; the lure of the outside world beckoned, but she knew she was safer where she was. She'd called her brother Sean during one of her visits back to the cottage to water her plants and pick up some painting supplies. The cops hadn't bothered him again, so hopefully it had all blown over and they no longer needed her to testify. Maybe Etienne had turned snitch. She'd always sensed something different about her ex-boyfriend. It was like he had some secret agenda.

"I want to go to the winery," Charles said as she shut off the engine in front of the chateau.

"Um, okay. Will your cart make it that far? Or can we borrow one of Jacques's cars?"

Charles shook his head. "No, I want to go on the bike. There's a road through the estate; we don't have to go on the highway."

"Didn't Jacques say he was going to the winery today? Are you trying to get me in trouble?"

She'd been aware of Jacques watching them through the window in the home office whenever they strolled through the rose garden. And he hadn't returned to Paris as expected. Instead he'd announced that he was going to work from the chateau for the rest of the summer. He clearly didn't trust her. At least he hadn't brought up the land in the last week— but the way he stared at her sometimes, it was as though he was fighting some kind of internal battle.

"Fun is where the trouble is," Charles replied.

Not her kind of trouble. "Your grandson doesn't think so."

"He's been buried by all the responsibility of this place. He hasn't been able to have fun in a long, long time. I think he's forgotten how. You could show him."

It wasn't the first time Charles had pushed her in Jacques's direction or tried to get her to empathize with him. "We're too different. I'm pretty sure Jacques doesn't appreciate my kind of fun."

Then again, what did she find enjoyable now? She didn't miss going to clubs or parties at all. Her good times were hanging with Charles, working on her art in the afternoon, and spending her nights imagining all the wicked things she'd like to do to Jacques in the next room.

"You'll never know until you try," Charles said.

She wasn't going to get anywhere arguing with him. "All right, I'll take you to the winery. But if I get sent to my room without supper, you have to promise to bring me something to eat through the secret passages."

"Of course."

She'd probably pay for this later. On the plus side, Jacques was unlikely to tell her off for putting Charles's life at risk with his grandfather there. Which meant that she and Jacques would have to be alone.

She kicked the Ducati back to life. *Fun, here I come.*

The Vintner and The Vixen

***

The deep rumble of Maya's motorbike pulled Jacques from his analysis of the tartaric acid levels in the wine they were preparing to bottle. Had something happened to Grand-Papa? No, someone would have called. And it had to be the momentary worry over his grandfather that accounted for the rise in his heart rate. Not Maya's arrival.

He put down his clipboard and went to the back door just in time to see Maya help Grand-Papa off the back of her bike. Did the woman have no sense at all?

With his thumb, he rubbed the bare spot where his wedding ring used to sit. Had Maya noticed that he'd taken it off? After her diatribe at the cottage, he'd tried to put the past behind him. Which admittedly was easier now that he had a whole new set of issues to deal with.

She pulled off her leather jacket, revealing another of those infernal tops that left her midriff bare so he could admire her taut abs and belly button ring. He'd never made love to a woman with a pierced navel.

Merde. He'd been doing so well in keeping the lust at bay, despite the fact that Maya didn't seem to own a dress with a back—or a hem longer than her upper thigh.

Princess flopped at his feet, her tongue lolling out. He tightened his lips before he wore the same expression as the dog. Maya raised her arms to refasten her ponytail, and her shirt rode up so that it barely covered the bottom of her breasts. To distract himself, he got a bowl of water for Princess.

"Hello, Jacques, we've come for a visit," Grand-Papa said after removing his helmet. Maya had a hand under his elbow, and she steered him toward the bench against the wall.

"So I see. You could have used one of the cars."

"I wanted a ride on Maya's Ducati. I haven't felt so alive in years. Have you ridden her?"

Maya tried to hide a smirk but failed.

Jacques's gaze caught hers and held it. "No, I haven't had the pleasure."

A faint pink hue stained Maya's cheeks. So, the bad girl could blush.

"You should try it some time," Grand-Papa insisted.

"I'll discuss that with Maya later." He forced his eyes back to his grandfather. He did look remarkably well. There was color in his cheeks and a huge smile on his face. His grandfather had found a new lease on life, thanks to Maya.

The maintenance invoice still sat on his desk, waiting for the appropriate time to present to her. Except that time never came. In the mornings she was out walking the gardens with his grandfather, her bubbly laughter filling the air and disturbing his peace of mind as he tried to work. In the afternoons she was in one of the salons, working on her art. He'd checked on her a couple of times and been amazed at the quality of her work. So he'd asked her to paint a picture of Grand-Papa, Daniel, and himself. It would make a perfect present for his grandfather on the next special occasion. It therefore seemed rude to give her a bill when she was working on a commission for him, one she'd refused to charge for on the grounds

85

that her room and board were payment enough.

Then in the evenings, they'd have drinks in the *petit salon* before enjoying a meal that often lasted more than two hours. When they talked so much, it took a while to eat. Grand-Papa would tell stories of before the war, Maya would tell tales of her Gran-Gran, and they'd both tease Jacques for never having gone camping or learned to ride a bike, or a million and one other, normal things that he'd missed out on.

To get them off his back, he'd bragged that he and Daniel had stolen the chef's baking pans one rainy day and tried to luge down the stairs. Maya had asked for a reenactment, and he'd admitted that he had a chip in his coccyx while Daniel had ended up with a cracked rib. It was unlikely they'd do it again.

"To what do I owe the pleasure of this visit?" His gaze automatically returned to Maya.

"I wanted to see how the latest vintage was coming along," Grand-Papa answered.

As far as he knew, his grandfather hadn't visited the winery in years. He was up to something again. But it was nice that he was at least feigning an interest in something Jacques was passionate about. "Come have a taste," Jacques invited.

"Have you done a wine tasting before, Maya?" Grand-Papa looked up at her as she took his arm and helped him across the loose gravel.

"Oh, yes. I recently had a private lesson. I'm a certified wine snob now." Her sexy laugh accompanied her statement.

"Jacques has an amazing palate. He can tell the blend of a wine from one sip."

Maya's eyes met his. "I had heard he was good

with his tongue," she said so low Grand-Papa was unlikely to have heard.

Now it was his turn to blush. He ushered them inside and called for one of the staff to set up a tasting in the private cellar. Grand-Papa excused himself to use the facilities, leaving Jacques alone with Maya for a moment.

"It was reckless of you to bring Grand-Papa on your bike. What if he'd fallen off? Something as minor as a broken bone can kill him at his age."

"I know, but he insisted, and I was extremely careful. When he looks at me with those blue eyes, I can't deny him."

Lucky Grand-Papa. "I have the same blue eyes. Can you deny me?"

She took a step closer, right into his personal space. The heat from her body and her seductive perfume enveloped him. "What do you want, Jacques?"

"You." The word was out before his brain engaged. He braced himself for a slap, but all he got was a wicked smile.

"I thought I was too dangerous." She traced his lips with her index finger. One finger and he was hard.

"I seem to have developed a taste for danger."

"I wonder what your refined palate will make of that." She stepped back as Grand-Papa entered the room.

His grandfather's gaze swept between the two of them, his smile widening as both Jacques and Maya pretended they hadn't been seconds away from ripping each other's clothes off.

"I think the bike ride took it out of me," Grand-Papa said. "I'll skip the wine tasting and head back home." Maya turned towards the door, but before she could take two steps, Grand-Papa continued, "No, Maya, you stay and try the wine. I'll drive Jacques's car back and take Princess with me. I don't think she should run back to the chateau in this heat. Jacques can return with you on your bike when you're done."

Jacques shook his head. "Very subtle, Grand-Papa. And I thought it was old ladies who were matchmakers."

"At my age, I don't have time to be subtle. Hand over your keys, Jacques. I'll take the road through the estate so you don't have to worry about me on the highway."

Yes, that's what I'm worried about. Not spontaneous combustion with Maya's incredible ass between my thighs.

He handed his keys to his grandfather, then waited reluctantly while the staff member set up the tasting. When he was alone again with Maya, he handed her a glass and watched while she swirled the liquid and examined its color.

"Sorry about my grandfather, dragging you over here."

"I don't mind. It's sweet how he thinks we should get together. I mean, I know it's because I'm the only woman around, aside from your staff. It's not like we're really suited or anything." She held the glass to the light. "This one's more of a magenta color."

"Why don't you think we're suited?"

She took several sips of the wine. "I'm getting

hints of cinnamon and maybe blackberries?"

"You haven't answered my question." He took the now empty glass from her hand.

"Oh, come on, Jacques. Aside from the 'you're a woman and I'm a man so seduction is always in the cards' thing, I am *so* not your type."

"What is my type?"

"Is this a wine tasting, or are you looking to set up an online dating profile?"

It was the first sign of nervousness he'd seen from her. He pressed his advantage. "What's my type, Maya?"

"Smart, sophisticated, elegant, maybe a little on the snobby side."

"You are all those things."

"Really? You think I'm a snob?"

"You freely admitted to being a wine snob earlier, and you've just expertly categorized my new vintage. But you left beautiful, sensuous, and funny off your list of qualities."

"Don't be ridiculous."

"I'm not. I've seen another side to you in the two weeks you've been at the big house. Your prickly pear outside hides a soft, squishy interior." A strand of her hair had sprung loose from her ponytail. He curled it around his finger before tucking it behind her ear. Did she just tremble at his touch?

"Well, you're still the same Jacques. Why haven't you asked me to sell you the land lately?"

He smiled. She thought throwing their unresolved dispute between them would stop him? This vulnerable Maya was new. Or was she playing him again? "I was waiting for the right opportunity."

"Then you're wasting your time. I won't sell."
She put her hands on her hips, which thrust her chest
out towards him. Putting his hands over hers, he
pulled her against him.

"So, where does that leave us?"

"At opposite sides of the boxing ring."

"Boxers are only on opposite sides of the ring at
the start of the match. They spend most of the bout as
close as we are now."

"Until one of them gets knocked to the ground."

"I'm not looking to knock you out, Maya. I just
want back what's rightfully mine."

"And that's where we disagree."

"There is one thing we can agree on."

"And what's that?"

"This passion between us." He took her lips in a
blistering kiss. Her hands escaped from under his to
roam up his chest and into his hair. The air
conditioning couldn't cope with the heat they
generated. They kissed until he was dizzy. Then he
forced his lips to release hers and moved to her ear. "I
forgot rule number two—no condoms."

"You are really rusty at this seduction thing,
aren't you?" She stepped back and fixed her hair,
which had tumbled down during their passionate
embrace.

"In my defense, I came to work. I didn't expect
you to show up and drive me insane." He buttoned
his shirt back up; it would be a couple of minutes
before he could tuck it in again.

"It's probably for the best."

"Maya—"

"Can you get a ride back to the house, Jacques? I

need some time alone to think."

He nodded, and she was out the door before he could even tell her to drive carefully.

Dieu, what was he going to do? Because at the moment he had only two options—kick her out of his life for good, or take her to bed.

Chapter 10

This was the do-or-die moment. Her grip tightened on the door handle to Jacques's room. All she had to do was push it open.

After fleeing the winery that afternoon, she'd ridden west until she'd hit the Atlantic. There, as vacationers enjoyed the hot summer day with ice creams, she'd taken off her boots and walked the beach, imagining that the water lapping her ankles had once been on the shores of Canada. She couldn't go back. And she couldn't go forward.

How could she even contemplate a relationship with Jacques, knowing that any second Tony, or the RCMP for that matter, could find her and either kill her or take her to jail?

But she couldn't stay at the chateau, or even at the cottage, without doing something. The chemistry between her and Jacques was too explosive to ignore. She had to either push him away or pull him closer. She knew which one her body wanted. Was it fair to offer him an affair with no future? Even without the price on her head, what real chance did they have? They were too different to make something permanent work. Besides, she wasn't ready to settle down yet.

She knew she had to return the land, and probably the cottage, to the de Launay family. It wasn't right for her to keep what had been in their family for centuries. As soon as she lived up to her promise to Gran-Gran to spend a year concentrating on her art, she'd make a deal with Jacques. Nothing like the 10 million euros he'd offered. Maybe just enough to get a small place in a neighboring village. There was nothing in Canada for her to go back to. Her life, for as long as she had one, was here now.

In the meantime, what should she do about Jacques? Maybe a short-term affair would clear the air of the lust-haze that enveloped them. Once they'd satisfied their passions, they could both go back to their original truce. Yeah, her body had definitely overruled her brain on that decision. On the way back to the chateau, she'd stopped at a pharmacy and bought the biggest box of condoms they sold.

So, here she stood, outside his bedroom dressed in her most seductive negligee, because when you renegotiate an agreement, you should do it from a position of strength.

The handle turned smoothly in her hand, the door opening with a slight *creak*.

There was a rustling noise from across the room and then a pool of light as Jacques sat up and turned on the lamp beside his bed. He blinked a couple of times, and his lips curled upward in a slow, sensuous smile. *How many women have fallen victim to that smile?*

But Maya was no victim. She wanted this.

"Do you need something, Maya?"

"I want to renegotiate our initial truce."

"Why's that?" She should have wiped that sexy smile off his face by walking back out the door then and there. Except the way his eyes devoured her body made her want his touch even more.

"Because it doesn't seem to be working."

"I agree. So what part, exactly, do you want to renegotiate?"

"I'd like to do away completely with rule one."

"The one about us not touching each other?"

"Yes. And I'm going to take responsibility for rule two." She plonked the box of condoms on the bedside table.

"I did have that covered, just not at the winery." He opened the drawer next to his bed to reveal three new-looking boxes of protection and a host of lubricants, including massage oil.

"There are a few additional terms."

"I'm listening." *By staring at her barely concealed breasts?*

"This is a short-term, thirty-day, sex-only affair. I don't own you, and you don't own me, although if you want to sleep with other women, I'd appreciate if you'd let me know."

"I won't sleep with other women."

"I don't expect expressions of love, and if you even once mention money, I'll slap your rich-boy face into tomorrow."

"No love, no money. Got it."

"And for thirty days, neither of us brings up ownership of the cottage or the land. Those things have nothing to do with this." She waved her hand between them. "This is just to get rid of the lust between us. Nothing more." *God, I sound like a tramp.*

"I have one question."

"Make it quick." She'd thought a discussion between two half-naked people would go faster than this.

"What if thirty days isn't enough?"

"Then I guess we renegotiate when the time comes."

"I agree to your revised truce agreement. How do we seal this? A handshake?" His blue eyes sparkled with a mix of amusement and desire. Great, another de Launay she wouldn't be able to deny. He reached for her hand and tugged her towards him. She couldn't resist.

But she'd be damned if she'd give up control.

"I noticed you rubbing the back of your neck at dinner. I don't want you to get a migraine. So lay down, face up, with your feet the other side of the bed. We'll start with a cranial massage."

He hesitated. "I want to touch you. I've been waiting weeks for this. For you to come to me."

"Later. My turn first." Because it wouldn't take much to push her over the edge, and she wanted to eke as much pleasure out of the moment as possible.

He moved to comply. "Are you always this bossy in bed?"

"A lot of the time." She began to massage his scalp and his eyes drifted closed, a low moan of pleasure escaping his lips. After making sure there was no residual tension in his neck, she asked him to turn over.

She grabbed the massage oil from his drawer and then straddled him. She'd just found a model for her next sculpture. Men's backs had always been challenging for her to recreate, but under her fingers she had perfection. Pouring some of the lubricant into her hands, she worked her way from his broad shoulders down his spine to his narrow waist, allowing her fingers to slip under his hip bone at the front. She eased off his boxer shorts. He wouldn't be able to lay on his stomach for much longer. She'd better be quick. Her hands slid down one leg and up the other. His moans of pleasure grew louder.

"Maya, please…"

"I like a man who begs. You can turn over now. Arms to the side."

He turned so fast she almost fell off the bed. "I'm not begging…" He reached for the hem of her baby doll nightie, but she grabbed his hands and placed them back on the bed. "Okay, I'm begging. I have to touch you, taste you, feel your body against mine. You're driving me insane."

"Not yet." She was having too much fun to relinquish control now. She sat back on her ankles and massaged his feet then worked her way up his legs, lingering on his upper thigh, gradually increasing her circles. A long moan escaped his lips as she touched him.

Her games were taking a toll on her as well. She was so desperate to have him inside her, filling her, that she could barely think. She let go of him long enough to grab the box off the bedside table. Ripping the condom packet open with her teeth, she rolled it on him and his eyes flew open. She lifted her hips up and lowered herself onto him. He was so big, it took a few seconds for her body to adjust. Pleasure zinged through every pore. Jacques still had his arms spread wide on the bed, giving her total control. It was almost as heady as the feel of him twitching inside her.

Their gazes locked as she began to move on him, slowly at first, but soon the ability to pace herself disappeared. Her nightie clung to her perspiration-damp skin, so she lifted it off. Her breasts bounced as she rode Jacques, her breath coming in pants. With a shout of triumph she climaxed, seconds before he followed her over the edge.

She collapsed on top of him, and finally his hands came off the bed and held her tightly against him, her breasts crushed against his chest, their bodies still fused. His cock twitched within her and her body responded by clenching around him.

"*Dieu*, Maya. You found every single one of my wild man buttons. You're in for a world of pleasure now."

She raised her head from his chest. The sexy smile was back, and his face was flushed with pleasure. This was how she should have drawn him while he slept on her bed at the cottage.

"I look forward to it." Then she kissed him.

He was right. Thirty days might not be enough.

***

Something weighed Jacques down as he floated to consciousness. He reached up to remove the object and encountered soft hair and a warm breast. This was how a man should wake up every morning. If it could still be considered morning. Dawn had been breaking when they'd both finally been satiated enough to fall asleep.

They'd made love four times. After Maya's display of dominance, he'd taken charge for the second round, making her orgasm twice before he'd entered her and then not allowing his body release until she'd come again with him inside her. After that it had been a free-for-all as they'd learned each other's bodies and found pleasure together. And he'd discovered three more tattoos—some scrollwork at the base of her spine, a cupcake on her hip bone that she particularly liked to be licked, and a fox on her upper thigh.

As intense as the sex had been, they'd also had fun, making each other laugh and playing games.

Between rounds three and four, Maya had made him take her down to the kitchen using the secret passages. They'd returned to his bedroom with purloined chocolate croissants but had been so covered in dust and cobwebs that they'd showered together. It was a good thing there was no one else in their wing of the house, because Maya was a very vocal lover, shouting encouragement and screaming her pleasure.

Jacques felt like a god. A very hungry god. It was going to take more than *pain au chocolat* to replace the calories he'd burned in the night.

Maya stirred on his chest and raised her beautiful face. Her cognac-colored eyes sparkled with satisfaction. "Good morning. How's your head?"

"Both are well, thank you."

"Such formality the morning after. Do I need to find your wild man buttons and press them again?"

"No, they're permanently disabled where you're concerned."

"At least in the bedroom … and the shower … and that cute little alcove downstairs beside the library…"

"I promise to ravage you again in all those locations. But first I need to eat."

She stretched her lithe body, sliding off him. He missed her warmth, and rather than get out of bed, he rolled to his side so he could watch her.

"As king of this castle, can't you get breakfast delivered? I'm not sure my legs work well enough to make it downstairs," she said.

"I'm not a king, just a *comte*-in-waiting. But I think that will rank me high enough to get breakfast brought to us." He grabbed his phone off the bedside table and sent a text to Marie, the housekeeper. When he put the phone down, Maya sat up, the sheet falling to her waist. She wasn't self-conscious about her body; it was one of the many things he admired about her.

"Hold on a sec, did you just say you're a *comte*? What's that? Some sort of aristocrat?"

"Grand-Papa is the current Comte de Vendee. I'll inherit the title when he no longer uses it." Even though his grandfather was ninety-five, Jacques still couldn't contemplate a time when the old man wouldn't be around. He'd been the one constant in Jacques's life through all the ups and downs. Especially the downs.

"I thought the French beheaded all their aristocracy."

"A few of us managed to survive. The title is purely historical. I have no authority, except maybe to get my breakfast delivered when I can't be bothered to get out of my bed after it's been invaded by a beautiful woman." She tilted her head to one side, staring at him. It was the oddest morning after he'd ever had. Not that there'd been a lot of them, especially since Clarisse's death. "What's the matter? Don't I live up to your expectation of a *comte*?"

"Can't say I have any expectations where *comtes* are concerned. The only counts I know are Dracula, Chocula, and the one on *Sesame Street* who helps kids with their numbers."

"I probably fall somewhere between the second and third one."

"Well, just in case, I'll be checking for bite marks on my neck. But I've seen you in the daylight, so I'm probably safe. What's your full name? Don't aristocrats usually have, like, hundreds of names?"

"Jacques Charles Henri de Launay. Not hundreds, only three. Sorry to disappoint."

She leaned down then and stopped with her lips hovering over his. "Let's get one thing clear, Jacques Charles Henri de Launay, next Comte de Vendee. You do not disappoint." She kissed him then, long and slow, her tongue and lips making love to his. His cock stirred to life, ready to take on the challenge of not disappointing Maya.

His hand found its way to her breast just as there was a loud knock at the door.

"I don't want to embarrass Marie," Maya said as she slid out of the bed. "I'll use the washroom while you get breakfast sorted." With a sassy smile and a wave, she disappeared into the adjoining bathroom.

By the time she emerged a few minutes later wearing a short satin wrap, he had breakfast laid out on the round table that had sat in the corner since he'd moved into the room five years ago. It had probably been there for centuries. He couldn't imagine either his mother or grandmother ever having breakfast ensuite after a night of pleasure. So it probably hadn't been used in generations. There were a lot of things the house hadn't seen in generations. Like laughter in the bedroom. Or a happy marriage. At least he could rectify one of those things.

He poured Maya a coffee and uncovered the platter with the omelet. "I ordered enough for two."

"Yum, thanks. Amazing how hungry a person gets after a night of fun."

"It's also eleven o'clock. So your body is probably missing breakfast."

"The only thing my body is missing is yours. But I'll let you eat first." She stole the toast he'd just buttered right out of his fingers, then looked around the room as if seeing it for the first time. "Your room is nice. How come it's not as badly decorated as the rest of the house?"

He buttered another slice of toast and took a mouthful before she had a chance to steal that one as well. "I don't think Clarisse ever set foot in here. The decor is left over from when my parents had the room."

"Your wife never set foot in your bedroom? Not even for a booty call?" She stared at him wide-eyed, her breakfast forgotten.

"She wasn't interested in sex. Thought it was too messy."

"Oh-my-God-she-didn't." Maya said it like it was one word.

He'd never opened up to anyone about his marriage before. But Maya made him want to confess the whole frigid affair so he could put it behind him. "Once, when I was trying something new, hoping to get Clarisse interested, I looked up to find she was texting her friend about a lunch date."

Maya whooped with laughter. Tears streamed down her face, and she banged her hand on the table, making the glasses and cutlery tinkle. He'd just told her his most embarrassing memory, and she'd laughed. He picked up his fork and stabbed the omelet. When only an occasional snort came from the other side of the table, he raised his eyes to hers.

"Oh, Jacques, Clarisse must have been a robot. There is no way her reaction was due to your lack of skill in bed. When we kiss, I can't even spell *text*. And when you go down on me, I can't remember my own name. But if it's any comfort, I don't have a cell phone. So feel free to experiment on me anytime."

The pressure in his chest released. Maya was about fun. He needed to let go of the past and learn to live in the moment. He had thirty days, and he was going to revel in every single second.

"Eat up, Maya. I'm feeling scientific."

Chapter 11

Maya tried to keep her mind on what Charles was saying, with little success. She couldn't concentrate on the history of the de Launay family when her body wanted to be wrapped around the current heir. Things had gone way beyond scratching an itch. It was now a full-blown addiction. Evidently, she'd found the drug that gave her a high: Jacques crack. Who knew?

Every few minutes she'd check behind her to see if he'd finished his conference call and was about to join them.

"He's an amazing man. He's just forgotten how to live. All he does is work," Charles said.

"Sorry, who?" She could feign ignorance. Charles was too astute, though, and laughed.

"My grandson. And you're the perfect woman to bring him back to life."

"Charles, this thing with Jacques and me—it's just a bit of fun. Don't get your hopes up for wedding bells and babies. I'm starting a new life, finally doing what I want for a change. I have absolutely no intention of settling down with any man," she said. Out of the corner of her eye she saw Jacques stride towards them. Her heart raced, and a shiver of anticipation flashed through her. That was not how it was supposed to be.

"I'm sorry to hear that, Maya. You are like your great-grandmother. She loved her independence, too." His mouth twitched down for a moment. "If you'll excuse me, I'm not feeling well. I think I'll lie down." He turned on his heel and headed off towards his bedroom, his head bowed, his feet shuffling more than usual.

Jacques hurried over to her. "Everything all right?"

"I think I just broke your grandfather's heart."

Jacques stared at his retreating grandparent. "How'd you do that?"

"I told him we were just having fun. That we would never get together permanently."

His gaze searched her face for a moment, his eyes unreadable. "Grand-Papa is worried about the end of the de Launay line. He's been after me to remarry for over a year now. And he's trying so hard to throw us together, I can see how he'd think he'd finally succeeded."

The giggle that should have accompanied his statement died in her throat. Who could imagine a girl from a trailer park with a history of drug-dealer boyfriends as the wife of a French nobleman?

"Well, I think we need to be a bit more careful so he doesn't get his hopes up further."

"As long as you don't expect me not to touch you when he's around. I don't think I have the willpower to resist the lure of your creamy skin." He trailed his fingers along her cheek and into her hair, drawing her face up to his as his lips descended.

"Say things like that and I might forget—" The rest of her sentence was swallowed in his kiss.

"If Grand-Papa has gone to lie down, maybe we should do the same," he whispered into her ear a few moments later.

Get out, get out now! her voice of reason screamed. Her desire for independence was rapidly losing ground to her lust for Jacques.

"As tempting as that sounds, I need to create. I'm going to get my sketchbook from the cottage and draw the rose your grandfather showed me the other day. It really is special. Such an amazing shade of pink, almost a blush really…" She was babbling but couldn't help it. She needed to get away from Jacques's magnetic personality and regain her composure.

She should never have opened that damn door last night. It was her very own Pandora's box. Except instead of all the bad things flying out, she'd been shown what could have been if she'd made different choices in life.

If she hadn't seen what she'd seen, if her life didn't depend on remaining invisible, then she could fight for the relationship that dangled so tantalizingly before her.

But Jacques didn't release her. He seemed intent on taking advantage of every minute of their thirty-day ceasefire. "Can I tempt you with a visit to the lake? You can sketch there. I could use some fresh air."

She sighed, her resistance dissolving like salt in boiling water. "If you want fresh air, can we take my bike?"

His inner struggle was clearly shown on his face. She knew he didn't like to give up control. But if there was to be any sort of balance in their relationship, as short as it would be, she'd have to draw the line somewhere.

"Will you drive safely?"

"With you, of course. I'm not reckless, especially when someone else's life is at stake."

His eyes searched hers. "And when it's only your own?"

"I have a lot to live for, and I know what it feels like to watch someone you love die. I wouldn't do that to the people I care about."

"Then I'll meet you in fifteen minutes at the cottage. Is that long enough for you to get ready?"

"Yup. Oh, and Jacques? Don't forget the condoms."

Passion blazed in his eyes, and he took the stairs two at a time. Maya hurried out through the sitting room door to grab her art supplies.

When she parked her bike by the lake, Jacques dismounted and pulled off his helmet. He'd held himself so stiffly for the whole trip it was like riding with a giant statue on board. Okay, a sexy statue. She'd driven slowly, to reassure him it was safe. That it meant more time with the power of the engine between her thighs and the even more powerful man at her backside was just a happy coincidence.

Of course, the downside to coming by motorbike was that she'd only been able to bring her small sketchpad and watercolor pencils. Jacques had brought a blanket to sit on, a Thermos, and two stainless steel mugs. At first he sat beside her, watching her draw. But when she finally put her sketchpad down and looked around, she noticed that he'd wandered off to examine the grapes on the closest vines.

As if sensing her gaze, he returned to stand

beside her. "Done?"

"Yes. Sorry it took so long. I didn't mean to ignore you. I should have warned you that when I'm in the zone, I wouldn't notice if a helicopter were hovering meters above my head."

"I don't mind. I'm amazed at your talent. Is there anything you can't do?"

"I'm no good at abstract art. Every time I try, it ends up looking like a person or a landscape."

"Well, if I set out to draw a person or landscape, it would look abstract. I have no artistic talent at all."

"Yes, but you have other talents." She let her eyes linger on his lips and saw him swallow. "Before we indulge those, I'm going to cool off with a swim. You coming?" She didn't wait for his reply to strip off her clothes and run into the water. The coldness was a shock against her hot skin, and she shrieked.

"You're going to have half my workers here if you make so much noise," Jacques said, his arms coming around her.

"It was colder than I expected."

"Come back on shore and let me warm you up." His seductive voice in her ear made her internal temperature rise.

"In a minute. I'm going to swim first." They frolicked in the water for half an hour. When she eventually splashed to shore, her teeth were chattering so badly she couldn't speak. Jacques emerged and joined her on the blanket. The sun, combined with his nearness, soon warmed her.

"You cheated—you've still got your underwear on."

"There are eels in that water. I wasn't going to

risk losing something valuable," he said.

"But now you're going to have to ride back with wet boxers."

"Not if I dry them off first." He pulled them off, wrung them out, and hung them from one of the handles on her motorbike. Even cold, he was a magnificent specimen. He poured some chilled wine infused with fruit from the Thermos and handed her a cup. His gaze on her naked body heated her further.

He lay down next to her again, his hand caressing her skin from her hip to her breast and back down. "You've told me the story of the words on your neck. Do your other tattoos have meaning? This cupcake"—he traced the ink with his finger, sending quivers of desire through her—"seems anomalous with your personality. Now, if it were a chocolate croissant, I'd understand."

"I had a boyfriend who called me *cupcake*. It was like I was just a bit of dessert to him, and I hated it, which only made him use it more. I got the tattoo to remind me to choose better in the future."

"Did it work?"

"Not really." Because after him came Victor, then Etienne, and she'd barely escaped that relationship with her life.

"And the fox?"

"My vixen? She's who I want to be—smart, resourceful, not afraid of the dark."

"And how's that working?"

"Not sure. On the one hand, I'm lying naked on the shore of a lake with a man I met only three weeks ago. On the other hand, I'm lying naked on the shore of a lake next to you. The jury's still out on that one."

"Let's see if I can sway the vote," he said, his lips on hers.

They made love like they had all the time in the world, like they were each committing the other's body to memory. She was used to frenzied passion or playful sex, but this was deeper, more meaningful. And it scared her.

What tattoo should she get after Jacques exited her life? She had an uncomfortable suspicion that no ink would be required. He'd leave his mark indelibly on her heart.

She lay spent on top of him. His hand swept up and down her back as though he couldn't get enough of touching her.

"I forgot when I agreed to this thirty-day affair that I have to go to Russia next week on business. Will you come with me?" he asked.

Tempting. But the reality was that she needed to stay hidden. If she went with Jacques, there was bound to be photos or speculation about who she was. Not to mention that if her passport was flagged by the Canadian government, they'd find her in an instant. It was safer if she stayed here.

"I'd love to, but I can't at the moment."

She could sense his disappointment. He rolled to his side, but held her against him. His eyes were guarded when they met hers. "Do you think I don't want to be seen with you?"

"Maybe it's the other way around." She tried for flippancy, but he wasn't having it.

"Maya."

"I just don't want to go, okay? I'll be bored out of my mind while you're working. I'd rather stay here and concentrate on my art. That is the reason I came to France." *Liar, liar, pants on fire.*

"Fine. But I don't leave for a few days. So if you change your mind…"

How she wished she could. She'd always wanted to go to Russia and see the Hermitage. Maybe one day. When she wasn't wanted by either a gangster, a government, or a sexy billionaire. A shiver wracked her body.

As she tugged on her jeans, her hand rubbed against her vixen tattoo. Even foxes got to have fun sometime. She'd just have to be smart enough not to get her heart involved.

Yeah, right.

***

She was surprised to hear voices she didn't recognize in the sitting room, where the family met before dinner. Were the de Launays having a dinner party? Should she go down to the kitchen and eat with the staff? She hesitated so long that Jacques caught sight of her through the open door.

"Maya, come in. Allow me to introduce you to Philippe Boudreau and his wife, Michelle. Philippe and Michelle, this is Maya, an artist from Canada who's come to stay at the cottage for a year." Jacques touched her arm briefly as he introduced her to the couple in their late fifties. The man was deeply tanned as though he spent his summer outside, and his hair was even lighter than Jacques's. The woman had a firm handshake and a friendly smile. Her dark hair was liberally salted with gray. "Philippe is the head vintner at the winery. I was supposed to meet with him this morning, but I got preoccupied with something else, so we agreed to hold our discussions over dinner. I hope you don't mind."

Sheer willpower kept her blush at bay. Still, she had to clear her throat before replying. "Not at all. I was fascinated when you gave me a tour of the winery the other week. I'd love to learn more about the business."

"If we let these two talk grapes, we won't get a word in ourselves," Michelle said with a laugh. "Tell me about your art, Maya. What is your specialty?"

"I've done mostly painting in oils and some sculpting with clay. But I want to work with wood while I've got the space."

"I have no artistic talent myself, so I am envious of those who do. Tell me, when you see a piece of wood or clay, do you already imagine the finished product that waits inside?"

Jacques handed Maya a glass of wine then moved away to talk privately with Philippe. But as she and Michelle had a pleasant discussion about art and some of the famous pieces at the Louvre, she sensed Jacques's eyes on her more often than not. Her skin warmed, and she wished she hadn't worn the fitted dress with the high neck. If he wanted to pretend that she was just an artist in residence, he had to keep his gaze under control.

Charles shuffled into the room, looking all of his ninety-five years. Maya's chest ached to see him so frail. The echo of Gran-Gran's last days reverberated through her. Her great-grandmother's skin had been so gray, her hands so cold, that despite the blankets

Maya piled on or how much she rubbed Gran-Gran's hands, it hadn't helped. An icy chill slid down Maya's back. She couldn't lose Charles now, too. Excusing herself from Michelle, she rushed over to him. Before she could help him to the sofa, one of the staff arrived to announce that dinner awaited them.

Taking Charles's arm, she walked with him into the dining room, and he leaned heavily on her. She should never have so frivolously dismissed his desire that she and Jacques get together. Maybe they could pretend for a while, give the old man some hope. Except that was likely to land her in even deeper trouble.

Jacques sat at the head of the table with Maya at his right. Charles was next to her and the Boudreaus sat opposite. Conversation at dinner centered on the upcoming grape harvest. Maya had always thought that you picked the grapes, crushed them, stuck them in a vat with some yeast, and waited for nature to do its thing. She was learning that it was much more scientific than that.

"I want us to hold a harvest festival. Like we did in my day," Charles said, his voice nostalgic.

Jacques paused for a moment. "Grand-Papa, there hasn't been a harvest festival in twenty years. I wouldn't know what to do even if I had the time to organize it. I'm off to Russia soon for two weeks, and by the time I return, the harvest will be underway and it will be too late to make arrangements."

"Maya can do it," Charles insisted.

All eyes turned on her. "I haven't even been to a grape harvest, never mind a festival for one. I have no idea what to do."

Charles put his hand over hers. "I can instruct you. Please, this is likely to be my last harvest. I'd like it to be the best."

How could she turn down a request like that? Jacques's eyes met hers. There was a catch in his voice when he spoke. "You still have several harvests left in you. And Maya has her art to work on; she's not here to cater to our whims."

I catered to a few of yours last night, Jacques. But let's not bring that up in polite company.

"Please, Jacques," Charles said, a hint of moisture in his blue eyes.

Maya's heart shattered. "I'll do it."

Charles went from frail and desperate to invigorated and triumphant in the blink of an eye. She'd been played. Masterfully.

"Seems like we're having a festival." Jacques did not look pleased.

Wait till he found out her motto was *go big or go home*.

Chapter 12

Jacques paced in his room, shoving a hand through his hair. His grandfather had played the trump card, and Maya had folded like an amateur. Grand-Papa had never hinted that he wanted to resurrect the harvest festival before. It must be a scheme to keep Maya near and part of the family. Worse, Jacques couldn't deny the thrill that raced through his veins at the thought. Twenty-nine days. He'd have to negotiate an extension for the time he was away.

He had no control where Maya was concerned. It was as terrifying as it was liberating.

Maya came through the connecting bathroom door, still fully dressed. She even had her shoes on. Not staying, then. Damn. She'd gotten all defensive at the lake when he mentioned her traveling with him. Had she sensed that his desire was about more than sex, that he enjoyed their banter, that she made him feel alive for the first time in years?

"We need to talk." *Dieu*, not that.

"Would you like a cognac?"

"No thanks, but go ahead if you want one. What are we going to do about your grandfather?"

"My grandfather?" She wasn't here to tell him last night had been a mistake and she was repealing the revised truce agreement? He poured himself a drink and took a quick swig.

"Yes. I think he's fixated on getting us together. You know him best. Should we play along and pretend to fall in love? Give him some peace for a while? Or should I pack my things and move back to the cottage so he knows this is going nowhere?"

"It's too hot to sleep at the cottage." His brain had ceased functioning at the thought of Maya leaving so soon. There was still a plethora of things he wanted to do with her.

"I can survive. Besides, I like it hot." She shrugged as if it made no difference to her.

He put his glass down, walked over to her, and stared into her mesmerizing eyes. Who needed cognac when he could drown in her gaze? "Don't think about my grandfather. Don't think about me. What do *you* want, Maya?" If she stayed, it had to be because she wanted to. Anything else was cheating. Although his body would argue otherwise.

She took a deep breath then leaned over and removed her shoes, tossing them under the breakfast table. "I want to stay."

His breath whooshed out on an audible sigh. "I was hoping you'd say that."

"And I want to stay here. In this room. With you. Do you have a problem with that?"

He reached out and caressed her cheek. His hand slid into her hair, drawing her closer. "I was hoping you'd say that, too."

"And seeing as there's so much room, I thought Princess could join us." The sentence ended with his lips on hers.

He nibbled his way across to her ear. "No way. There are things I want to do to you that Princess might misunderstand. When you scream my name in pleasure, I don't want your dog to attack me."

She leaned back and stared into his eyes. "Intriguing. But I don't do bondage. Once you've been handcuffed and tossed into the back of a cop car, the titillation goes out of being restrained."

"I'm not into that either. I prefer full partner participation."

"Then I think we have a deal. Will you help me out of my dress?"

"It will be my pleasure."

"Our pleasure," she said as she spun around, presenting her back to him.

He slid the zipper down the back of her dress, undoing the hooks of her bra on the way, because he was efficient like that. Within seconds she stood before him, wearing only a black, lacy thong. He reached out to touch her, but she backed away.

"Your turn. Give me your best Magic Jacques impersonation."

"What?"

"Strip for me. Preferably to music."

She sauntered over to the bed, exaggerating the sway of her hips as she removed her thong. When she lay back against the pillows in her glorious nudity, he swallowed. "I don't have any music up here."

"Not even on your phone?" She lifted her hair off her shoulders and let it fall again before stretching her arms out wide. He couldn't take his eyes off her full breasts. A lock of hair curled around an already taut nipple. *Dieu*, this woman was going to be the death of him.

"It's a piece of business equipment. Not an entertainment device." His brain scrambled for options. The sooner he satisfied her demand, the sooner he could join her on the bed, sink into her delicious heat, and lose the precious little bit of his mind that still remained.

"I hope I don't fall asleep before you get here," she said. She stretched again, a huge fake yawn contorting her face.

He grabbed the TV remote, found the music channel, and scrolled through the selection. A trickle of trepidation ran through him. What if she laughed? But remaining uptight around Maya wasn't an option. He wanted this affair between them to be fun, something to look back on and smile. So, if he was going to do this, he was going to do it epically.

He chose 'Uptown Funk' and pressed play. His hips bopping to the beat, he danced like he hadn't done since he was ten years old—if then. She giggled as he licked his finger and then touched his ass with a sizzling sound. But it was encouragement, not derision. The sound of her provocative laugh emboldened him, and he strutted in front of her, giving the performance of a lifetime. It was damn hard to undo buttons when shimmying your shoulders. He had a new respect for strippers. Of course, they had Velcro on their side.

As he tossed his shirt to Maya, she sat up in the bed, her gaze riveted on him, biting her bottom lip seductively. Her skin was flushed, a clear sign she was turned on. The awkwardness he expected from dancing in front of her had evaporated after the first chorus. Adrenaline, passion, humor—they all combined to heighten the pleasure in the moment. If he'd been told a month ago that he'd strip in front of someone and enjoy it, he wouldn't have believed them.

When he was down to his boxers and the song was nearing its end, he turned his back to her, then moved his ass in circles as he lowered his shorts centimeter by centimeter. Maya yelled and clapped as though he were Channing Tatum. When the last note played, he spun on his heel and spread his arms wide, revealing all. *Dieu*, the hot look in Maya's eyes set his skin on fire.

"I knew you had it in you. Now I need *you* in *me*," she said, her voice husky.

But he wasn't done. He'd worked his clothes off, so he wanted more than just a quick tumble. This was a night he wanted her to remember for a long time. "Not just yet. I performed for you. I at least deserve a massage for all my hard work."

"Absolutely. Lay down. I'll get the oil." She went to move off the bed.

"No, I get to massage you. And this time, you have to keep your hands off me. Think you can manage that?"

Her gaze raked him. He might have overestimated his ability to stay in control.

"Go ahead, make me say your name."

"By the time I'm done, you'll be screaming it," he promised.

And she did, multiple times. Later they lay in an exhausted tangle of limbs while the air conditioning cooled their sweat-slicked skin. Sex had never been this amazing. Anyone after Maya was going to be a huge letdown.

Merveilleux*, Jacques. First you marry a woman who destroys your faith in that institution. Then you* *take a lover who ruins you for any other.* He could picture his grave marker: Jacques Charles Henri de Launay, Comte de Vendee: celibate, miserable, end of the line.

At least he'd be able to look back with a smile on his time with Maya. The trick would be to make it last as long as possible. Getting the land back was about to take second place to keeping the woman. More importantly, he had to make sure his heart stayed clear of the negotiations.

***

Jacques put down the phone and scrubbed a hand over his face. He'd known the party would end soon, but he'd hoped to make it last until his trip to Moscow at the end of the week. But now he had to fly to Tallinn first, and he needed to leave early in the morning. Twelve more hours with Maya. How many of them could they spend in his room?

Except Maya was so busy organizing this *maudit* festival that she barely had a moment during the day for a stolen kiss. Although yesterday he had done her on the desk when she'd come in to ask him about the budget.

His desire for her was off the charts, or the hook, or the chain, or whatever the current slang was. Maybe this business trip would give him some perspective. He could take a step back and see the situation rationally. Regain control. More likely than not, however, he'd find out how painful it would be to go cold turkey from his Maya addiction.

He'd find her now and tell her about his revised

travel plans. Maybe they could have a private dinner together. Grand-Papa would understand. He'd probably send up a bottle of champagne from his personal collection.

As Jacques exited his office, the first person he encountered was his grandfather.

"Jacques, Maya has had the most fantastic ideas for the festival. This is going to be an amazing year." Grand-Papa was vibrating with excitement, his eyes bright, a huge smile on his face.

Dieu, when this ended he wasn't sure who was going to take it the hardest, him or his grandfather. "Grand-Papa, don't put too much pressure on Maya. She's not a professional event planner. Let's just get this year under our belt, and then we can learn for future festivals."

"You need to have more faith in your woman, son."

Jacques closed his eyes. This had to stop. "She's not my woman. You have to get it out of your mind that we're a couple. She has her life, I have mine. They're intersecting for a brief time, but soon she'll leave, we'll have our property back, and we can all go back to normal."

"I don't like normal," Grand-Papa said, shuffling away.

Jacques turned to find Maya a few feet away, her face pale, the smile on her face faker than a Louis Vuitton bag at the market. She had to have overheard his last statement to his grandfather. He'd broken her rule about mentioning the land. Would she cancel the truce?

"Maya." His voice turned husky just uttering her

name.

"Hi, I … um … just wanted to check if it's okay if I redecorate the ballroom for the festival. Nothing major, just a bit of paint and reorganizing the furniture. I'll need to start now, though, if it's to be done in time for the party." She stared over his left shoulder. Her eyes, when they did flicker to his face, were sad.

"Do anything you want. Have the painters or contractors send the bill to me. I trust your judgment." He ran his hand through his hair again. Where had the impeccable control freak gone? What next? Was she going to turn him into the irresponsible waster his father had been? This business trip was coming at just the right time to regain his perspective. Until then, however… "I was coming to tell you that I have to travel to Estonia tomorrow morning. How about we have a private dinner together? Then you can tell me about all your plans without Grand-Papa interrupting with more suggestions."

"Sounds lovely, but I promised to have dinner with Michelle Boudreau at her house. She's helping me, as she knows all the local businesses."

Disappointment smothered him, making it hard to breathe. "Can't you meet with her tomorrow?"

Maya touched his cheek briefly, but where the day before the caress would have been followed by a kiss, today she stepped back. "We have to make several critical decisions tonight so we can sign contracts tomorrow."

"I'll wait up for you, then."

"Whatever." And with that she was gone.

Chapter 13

Maya surveyed the ballroom. The robin's egg blue walls and cream trim worked well with the splashes of burgundy she'd chosen as an accent color. She'd scoured the chateau and replaced the gold-painted furniture with dark wood pieces and moved the mirrors so they bounced light rather than blinded. Two weeks from today the room would be full of people, only a handful of whom she knew, celebrating an event she'd never been a part of. But with Michelle's help, it was all coming together nicely.

They'd decided on a vintage theme for the ball, going back to the 1930s, before the war that had changed the family's fortunes. Maya still had no idea what she was going to wear to the formal party. Nothing in her wardrobe was suitable, but she didn't have the time or inclination to travel to Paris to go shopping. Hopefully, she'd be able to stay in the background and direct things from the sidelines. No one need even know she was there.

It was the lull before the storm. Everything was arranged; all that remained was to fight the inevitable fires on the night. Right now her fingers itched to create. Organizing the festival had kept her so busy for the past two and a half weeks that she'd barely had time to miss Jacques.

What a lie.

She'd missed him every second. She'd checked

her watch at least every thirty minutes to see how close she was to their nightly video conference call. And to add to her misery, she still slept in his bed. If you could call tossing and turning for hours sleeping.

Each morning she'd wake to coffee and a *pain au chocolat* on their breakfast table in the room. Jacques had said he'd left a standing order with Marie to bring it up for her.

"Aren't you worried I'll get fat?" she'd asked him.

"I don't care what you weigh," he'd replied with a typical Gallic shrug. "I just want you happy."

But she hadn't had time to get fat either. She'd been too active lifting dust covers and searching through attics and forgotten rooms. Had she been an antiques dealer, she would have had an orgasm at all the gorgeous, long-forgotten pieces she'd uncovered.

In her search for furnishings to redecorate the rooms for the festival, she'd discovered an emerald-colored bedspread and had the housekeeper change it for the overly ruffled one in Clarisse's old room. The space was much less girly now, but for some reason Maya couldn't bring herself to sleep in the bed where Jacques had made love to his wife—even if the sex *had* been disappointing.

And there she was, thinking about him again. Damn, the man had invaded every part of her. She had to reclaim herself before she had nothing to go back to when, as he'd said, their lives no longer intersected. It was still all about the land for him. And for her? Well, she wasn't so sure what it was about anymore. Fun was morphing into more, and that was unsettling.

The Vintner and The Vixen

They were like two people waiting at the same station for trains in different directions. Eventually they'd part, but the key was to enjoy their time as much as possible while still keeping their ultimate destinations in mind. Hers was supporting herself as an artist. And unless she got some pieces to show, that wasn't going to happen. The log at the back of the cottage couldn't carve itself.

She found Marie Dubois in the kitchen, fussing over Princess. At first Maya had felt guilty about abandoning her new pet with Jacques's staff. But Princess had been supremely happy and spoiled rotten. Would the dog even come back to the cottage with her now?

That was one worry she needn't have bothered with, she thought as Princess raced ahead of her. She'd been back a few times since she'd moved up to the big house, but mostly just to water her plants and check on things. She'd have to remember to get air conditioning installed before the next summer. If she were still here next summer. Her brother Sean hadn't heard anything more about the trial, and she'd been too afraid to search the Internet for any information. So she was living in blissful ignorance. Or at least it would be blissful when Jacques returned.

After opening all the doors and windows to air out the cottage, she wandered out to the eight-foot-tall log she'd been working on weeks ago. She circled the massive piece of wood three times, stopping to view it from different angles. When she'd bought it, she'd envisaged carving a woman ensnared in grape vines. She'd thought maybe Jacques might want it for the winery. But she could no longer see that. She sat on the lounger, the same one where Jacques had kissed her senseless the night he'd taught her to taste wine.

Oh God, no. Not that. Why did her muse taunt her with the impossible? Because as clear as if the sculpture were already done, she saw a man with his arms around his pregnant wife. And now that she'd seen it, she could see nothing else. Would Jacques think she was taunting him with an image from his past? Or a vision for the future?

Her arms burned from wielding the heavy chainsaw two hours later when Princess's sharp bark alerted her to the arrival of a visitor. Had Jacques come home early? Her heart leapt. She shut off the chainsaw and clambered down from the ladder.

But rather than the tall, muscular form of her lover coming around the corner, the smiling face of her new friend appeared.

"Hello, Michelle. Were we supposed to get together? Sorry, I completely forgot."

"No, we had nothing scheduled. I've brought someone to meet you. I would have called first, but at the chateau they said you were here and didn't have a phone."

"No problem. Is it someone who wants to be involved in the festival?" They already had everything arranged; accommodating another exhibitor was going to be a pain. But she didn't want to upset anyone.

"It's my mother-in-law. I told her about the festival and about you. Evidently, she was your great-grandmother's best friend. She insisted on coming right away to meet you."

"I'd love to meet her." Maya stripped off her coveralls and hard hat and followed Michelle around to the front of the cottage. There in the passenger seat of the car sat an old lady, a huge cardboard box in her lap.

"She's too frail to get out of the car, so if you don't mind talking to her there…"

"Not at all."

Michelle introduced them, yelling Maya's name. "She's deaf as a doorpost but too vain to wear hearing aids," Michelle explained.

"You have Yvette's eyes," Madame Boudreau said after searching Maya's face.

"And her sense of humor, too, I'm told. I didn't know Gran-Gran still had friends here, or I would have come to visit."

"Michelle was telling me about this festival you're organizing. I told her the best one the family had was when Yvette and Charles announced their engagement. It was a magical evening. People spoke about it for years."

"Even more after Yvette left, I imagine."

"Yes, that was a dreadful shame. Charles's mother was so horrid to poor Yvette and convinced her that the best thing for Charles and the family would be if she left France and never came back. Madame de Launay even offered Yvette money, but she wouldn't take it. Stupid, meddling old woman. She ruined two lives."

"Are you sure? I thought Gran-Gran left because she fell in love with my great-grandfather." Maya tried to connect the new information to what she knew of her great-grandparents' marriage. Her great-grandfather had been a gambler who'd disappeared shortly after her grandmother had been born. Maya assumed Gran-Gran hadn't talked about him much because she'd been embarrassed—not because she hadn't really loved him.

"That was the gossip the de Launays spread. But I knew it was because they never approved of Yvette. Not that it mattered to Charles. He loved her so much. He didn't care that she was the local baker's daughter. But his family wanted him to marry money, as they were going through theirs faster than they could make it. The whole estate was on the verge of bankruptcy."

"Truly, Mama? I never heard any of this," Michelle said as her mother-in-law paused for a labored breath.

"It was before your time, *chérie*. My father, like my son, ran the winery. So I knew about the years the staff went with little or no pay, only staying on because they had food and a place to sleep at night."

"My great-grandmother was a feisty woman. I don't think she'd let Charles's mother scare her off." Maya shook her head. She'd often sensed there was more to Gran-Gran's story. Madame Boudreau's frail hand reached for Maya's. It was so like her great-grandmother's that Maya blinked back a tear. She missed her so much.

"Yvette left," Madame Boudreau continued, "because she was convinced it was the best thing for the family. She said that eventually guilt for choosing her over the chateau would destroy Charles. But if he married the woman his parents wanted him to, the estate would be saved. It broke her heart, but there was no talking her around once she'd made her decision. Charles doesn't know. I debated for years whether to tell him but decided to let sleeping dogs lie. His heart was broken after Yvette left. Knowing the truth wouldn't have made a difference." Madame Boudreau let go of Maya's hand and wiped a tear from her own eye. Her chest rose and fell rapidly. Even this little talk seemed to have winded the elderly lady.

Charles had told her things had been difficult, but Maya hadn't realized the family had been on the verge of insolvency. And then to have his love leave him, allegedly for another man. At least Jacques had turned around the family fortunes, although his score in the love department seemed to be as bad as his grandfather's. Inadvertently, the de Launays' financial problems had been solved at the expense of love. Was there a way to redress the balance? Show them the way back to love?

Oh God. She wasn't falling in love with Jacques, was she? It was supposed to be a bit of fun, two trains and all that. Her hand shook as she tucked a strand of hair behind her ear.

Madame Boudreau tried to lift the big box on her lap, her thin arms shaking under the weight. "This is Yvette's engagement dress and shoes. She'd saved all her money for a year to buy it. She gave it to me before she left for Canada. Said she'd never wear it again. But I think you should have it."

Maya struggled not to cry as she took the white box from Michelle's mother-in-law. She lifted the lid and that was it. The tears streamed down her face, although she was careful to keep them from falling onto the navy blue satin. One last present from Gran-Gran.

"It's in good condition," Michelle said. "Will you try it on? Mama would love to see it on you."

Maya nodded, not trusting her voice to work. She went into the house and lifted the beautiful gown from the box. It had been lovingly preserved, and there wasn't a stain or tear on it. Racing upstairs, she quickly changed. She couldn't believe it fit. Well mostly. Maya's boobs were a little more exposed than was probably considered appropriate back in the 1940s. It was a halter-neck, backless, and fell in soft folds from her hips to pool around her feet. Two light blue panels of the sheerest silk hung from her shoulders down the back. It was elegant, sexy ... and priceless, because it had belonged to the woman she'd loved. She wiped her eyes and then put on the delicate, strapped shoes.

Gran-Gran must have been so happy when she'd worn the dress. Maya was on the edge of happiness but too scared to take it. What if Big Tony found her? She'd have to leave, maybe even without explaining why. Would Jacques be upset if she left as suddenly as her great-grandmother had? They'd agreed to a thirty-day affair, although he'd skillfully negotiated an extension to account for the time he was away. Would he want more? Could she give him more, knowing her heart was becoming involved?

Maya returned to the car to show the Boudreaus, making sure the small train from the dress didn't drag on the pebble drive.

"You are as beautiful as Yvette," Madame Boudreau declared. "You must wear it to the harvest festival."

"But won't that upset Charles?" The dress was perfect. And she'd like to look nice for Jacques. But not at the expense of Charles's feelings.

"Men rarely remember what a woman wore," Michelle said. "And knowing Charles, even if he recognizes the dress, he'll be pleased to see it on another woman he cares for."

Maya simply nodded, unable to form another word. This dress was the symbol of her great-grandmother's sacrifice. Evidence of a love so deep, she'd given up her own happiness to ensure the one she loved was better off. Did Maya have that kind of love in her? Michelle's voice brought her back to the moment.

"When the festival is finished and you have more time, Mama would like you to come and visit. She has lots of stories of your great-grandmother to share."

Maya smiled through her tears. "I'd love that. I miss Gran-Gran so much. It would be fabulous to talk to someone else who knew her as well."

Michelle got back in the car, and, after exchanging kisses through the window with Madame Boudreau, Maya waved them goodbye.

She now had the dress. Would the evening bring her love? Or heartache?

Chapter 14

Jacques scanned the faces at the airport, searching for his driver. Instead Daniel stood there, wearing a chauffeur hat and carrying a sign with Jacques's name on it. His brother's antics made him smile. But the warmth coursing through him had more to do with the knowledge that in half an hour he'd have his arms around Maya. Ten minutes after that he hoped to have her naked body pressed against his. That was the homecoming he wanted after sixteen nights away.

"You moonlighting?" Jacques asked as Daniel reached for his bag.

"Grand-Papa sent me."

"Is he okay? Is Maya okay?" Jacques scanned his brother's face, a trickle of fear replacing the warmth of a minute ago. *Dieu*, what if Maya had crashed on that motorbike of hers? She drove it too fast, and there wasn't even a scrap of metal to protect her. His stomach churned. He couldn't go through that again.

"Both are fine," Daniel replied quickly. "We want to talk to you about Maya."

They exited the airport and Daniel directed him towards his Mercedes parked as far away from all the other cars as possible. "What about Maya?"

"According to Grand-Papa, you're having an affair."

Jacques shrugged. He wasn't a man to kiss and tell. Or as it was with him and Maya, have multiple off-the-chart orgasms and then brag about it. "Is that what you want to talk about, my relationship with Maya?"

He wasn't sure he wanted his brother's or grandfather's interference. What he and Maya shared was too explosive to involve other parties.

"In a way. We're concerned that you'll let your experience with Clarisse stop you from letting Maya into your heart."

Jacques stopped walking. Really? Relationship advice from the world-famous playboy who'd never had more than two dates with the same woman? "First, it wasn't an 'experience with Clarisse'—it was a god-awful marriage. Second, I want Maya in my bed, not my heart."

Daniel laughed and carried on walking, so Jacques had to jog to catch up with him or take a taxi home. The taxi was looking like the better option at the moment.

"That ship has left the harbor, *mon frère*. You may think you're just banging her, but that woman is so deep inside you, you don't know where you finish and she starts."

"You're a prick, do you know that?"

"So I've been told. But the word coming down from Grand-Papa is it's time to move on and give Maya the chance she deserves."

"She takes risks—drives that bike of hers too fast and climbs ladders with a heavy chainsaw—how can I live with that? Knowing she could be hurt or killed? I can't go there again." It was the shallowest of the deep, dark places he didn't want to revisit, but Daniel didn't need to know that.

"Maya takes risks because she has nothing to

lose. I'll bet you anything that once she knows you feel something more for her than lust, she'll be extra careful because she won't want to worry you."

"I don't know. She's a wild child; she's lived her life on the edge."

"And that's why you're the perfect couple. You can teach her control. And she can help get rid of that pole you've got shoved up your ass. Don't let your woman slip away like Grand-Papa did. Hold on to her, Jacques."

"Maya and I can't live the life that Charles and Yvette should have had."

Daniel let loose a frustrated sigh. "He doesn't want you to live the life he wanted. He wants you to live the life you deserve. A life with a good woman at your side and a house full of children to keep you from forgetting what's really important: family."

"No child can replace the one I lost. You don't just forget something like that." Jacques shut down the horrific memory of staring into Clarisse's dead eyes, knowing he'd never look into his son's.

"I'm not asking you to forget it. I'm asking you to cherish the memory and find a way forward. Don't let Clarisse destroy your future as she's done your past. You can still have a family, Jacques. Marry for love *and* for lust this time."

"I'm a long way from considering marriage. But I'll think about what you said." It'd be right up there on his to-do list, just below getting his prostate checked.

"Good. My job is done. Now I just have to drive you home, say hi to Grand-Papa, and kiss Maya. Then I can get back to a very interesting blond who's waiting for me in Paris."

"In that case, I'll save you one step and kiss Maya for you."

Daniel laughed again and Jacques gritted his teeth. It had been a while since he'd punched his brother in the face, but he was coming mighty close now.

"See, you've got it bad, brother. Might as well get measured for my wedding tux now."

"Shut up and drive."

***

Jacques's chest tightened incrementally as he searched for Maya. She'd not been in the hallway with his grandfather. Maybe Grand-Papa had asked her to wait elsewhere so he could ascertain how the conversation with Daniel had gone. But after a quick welcome home, his grandfather had gone off to watch some TV show in his room, leaving Jacques to find Maya.

He checked the ballroom first; maybe she was already setting up for the party and lost track of time. But aside from an amazing transformation, the room was empty. Next up was the *petit salon* where they always met for drinks before dinner. He stood for several minutes just admiring the changes. It had gone from over-the-top ostentatious to warm and comfortable. A room a family could enjoy. The walls were painted in an ombré style, starting off a warm reddish-pink before brightening to a soft yellow, like sunrise turning to day. Photos of him and Daniel as children and adults now adorned the top of the drinks cabinet and other surfaces. The uncomfortable furniture had been replaced with stylish pieces that invited a person to relax. There was even a dog bed tucked into the corner. But no dog. And no Maya.

The ache in his chest grew stronger. He now had a home fit for a family. All he needed was the family.

Was she waiting for him in his room? During their nightly video chats, she'd lounged in his bed, often wearing the most seductive lingerie he'd ever seen. After each call, he'd had to take a very long, cold shower to even manage a few hours of sleep. He took the stairs two at a time. The disappointment when she wasn't there hit him like a TGV train at full speed.

Having looked in all the likely locations for Maya, he finally asked Marie, who told him she'd moved back to the cottage. Had Maya bored of him already? Moved on because he'd been gone for more than two weeks? During their calls they'd flirted and teased, but it wasn't the same as being with her. Maya had told him about the preparations for the festival and asked him at length about his business trip, pretending to be very interested in what he was doing. Maybe she'd felt uncomfortable staying at the house when he wasn't there. He would convince her that she belonged at the chateau.

She belonged.

Perhaps Daniel was right. It was time to let go of the past and move forward. Jacques jogged the last fifty meters to the cottage. He knocked at the door, but there was no answer. Maya's motorbike was parked out front, so chances were she was at home. He went around the side of the cottage, calling softly to Princess so he didn't startle the dog.

Princess ran up to him and nuzzled his hand, expecting a pat. He fondled the dog's ears and then resumed walking. It was Princess's owner he really wanted to greet.

The first thing he saw on rounding the corner was a two-meter tall wooden statue. The back of a shirtless man was all he could see, the contours of the muscles so lifelike he was in awe. At the front of the statue, he gasped. The man had his arms around a pregnant woman, their hands intertwined on her extended belly. The woman's head was tilted back and she was staring up at the man in love. The man looked down at her with amazement in his eyes. The piece was so detailed, the emotion so evident, Jacques locked his knees to keep from running away. Maya was an incredible artist.

But why had she chosen to create this scene of domestic bliss in wood? Instead of the sharp stab to the chest at the reminder of all he'd lost, there was a fluttery feeling, as though a butterfly had emerged from its cocoon and was testing its wings. The future beckoned.

But first he had to find Maya.

He spun on his heel at a soft snuffling sound and found her lying on the lounger. Her hair was a halo of claret against the white fabric of the chair, framing her beautiful face. A chisel lay on the paving stone as if it had fallen from her open palm. As he stepped closer, he could see wood shavings scattered throughout her hair and on her clothes, and a couple of nicks on her hands. She looked so at peace, he couldn't wake her. No matter how much he longed to hold her and kiss her hello.

He pulled up a chair and sat where he could admire both the art and the artist. Each time he looked at the carving, he saw another detail: the rings on both their left hands. For all her talk about wanting just a short fling, did she long for a deeper, more committed relationship? The light landed oddly on the belly of the woman and he moved closer. There was an extremely faint outline of a baby's tiny foot on the abdomen. That incredible precision sent a shiver through him. He ran a finger over the tiny bump and closed his eyes at the flood of emotion it generated. He swallowed down the lump in his throat and caressed the tiny footprint one last time.

He'd wait for Maya at the chateau and leave her a note to come up when she woke. But as he turned to find a pen and paper in the cottage, her eyelids fluttered open. She blinked twice before a beatific smile curved her lips. *Dieu*, she was beautiful. There was no way on this planet he could stop from smiling in return. Maya had brought happiness and laughter back into his life. He was going to put everything he had into making this relationship succeed—push aside his fears and fight for what he wanted. If it didn't work, he could at least say he tried. If it did, he'd have gained the greatest prize ever: Maya.

***

Damn, she must have been more exhausted than she thought, because now she was hallucinating. Jacques was staring at her like the man in the sculpture. Sure, she'd created the man in his image. She'd even

137

carved the back muscles by embracing the sculpture from the front, inspired by the hours she'd spent running her hands over Jacques's muscular torso. But she'd been careful not to transfer his actual face onto the wooden sculpture. Nor hers. That would be too obvious.

"Hi." He dropped to his knees next to her lounger and placed his hand on her cheek.

He was real. Real and more gorgeous than she remembered. Had he always had those crinkles beside his eyes when he smiled?

"Hi back." As far as scintillating conversation went, theirs was pathetic. But hey, she'd just worked twenty-two hours straight on the sculpture—thanks to the powerful floodlights she'd borrowed from the chateau—before literally falling onto the lounger. It would take a while for her brain to start functioning again.

"Your piece is amazing. Breathtaking. What do you call it?"

Desire? Fantasy? You? "Future Perfect."

"It fits. I've missed you, Maya." He bent and kissed her lightly before trailing his lips across her cheek to her ear. She was acutely aware that she was a complete mess; it had been at least thirty hours since she'd showered, and her breath smelled like the million cups of coffee she'd drunk to finish the project once she'd started. She'd never had such an obsession to complete a piece—unless you counted her compulsion to imprint Jacques's taste and feel onto her body. Speaking of which…

"I missed you, too. But I need a shower before I can show you how much."

138

"Sounds like a plan."

He lifted her in his arms and carried her into the house, firmly telling Princess to stay when she started to follow them upstairs. After flicking on the water, he then returned and undressed Maya, stopping every few seconds to caress her skin. She returned the favor, removing his clothes piece by piece. By the time they entered the shower, her skin was so on fire from his touch that she wasn't sure if the water would put out the flames.

Despite sixteen days of abstinence, they made love slowly, rediscovering each other's bodies, prolonging the pleasure. When at last Jacques entered her, the beauty of the moment formed tears in her eyes. Sex had never made her cry before. Thank God the shower hid the emotional outburst. The last thing she wanted was to scare him off. Maya Tessier, destroyer of men, falling for the next Comte de Vendee.

Oh, Gran-Gran, I can't follow in your footsteps. I'm not strong enough to give him up, even though I could ruin the family. If Big Tony finds me...

"What you do to me, Maya," Jacques said into her ear. His voice was husky, with a note of tenderness. It might have been the exhaustion, but something had changed about him since his return. Had he really lowered the drawbridge so she could walk across the moat and into his heart? His eyes met hers as they climaxed together. Oh God, it was so real.

When he finally slid from her body, she clung to him, not wanting him to leave. "I don't think I can stand."

The Vintner and The Vixen

He scooped her in his arms, waited while she grabbed the towels off the rack, and carried her through to her bedroom. He wrapped her hair in a towel then laid her on the bed. With another towel he started to dry her, but when he got to her chest, he replaced the towel with his tongue, swirling patterns over her breasts, licking drops of water from her hardened nipples. She was floating on a cloud of desire; Jacques was the only thing in her world. It was more than enough.

This time there was no holding back. Jacques pleasured her until she screamed his name and came twice, hard, the self-satisfied grin on his face evidence that he wanted to control her body, make her his in every way possible.

"Whatever it is you do to me, don't ever stop," Jacques said when they both could speak again. He lay on his side, tracing lazy patterns on her collarbone with his finger. She nodded dumbly, unable to get the words past the lump in her throat. It wasn't a declaration of love, but he was obviously thinking of their relationship beyond thirty days.

Her eyes drifted closed. The stress of organizing the festival, her obsession with completing the sculpture—they all culminated in this one moment of pure bliss.

For now, it was enough.

Chapter 15

Maya stretched. A girl could get used to this. Super-sexy man in bed next to her. A bevy of staff to cater to her every whim. Her days busy but not overwhelming. No worries about paying the rent. Yup, she was living the life. Except she knew it wouldn't last.

Jacques had made no further mention of the future, but every day he seemed more relaxed, spending more time doing the things he enjoyed—including her—rather than being wrapped up in his business. He'd gone back to Paris for only three days since his return from Russia, and he'd come home each night, claiming he couldn't sleep apart from her. It was more likely that he was making the most of his enthusiastic sex partner. But since she slept so much better spooned against his body after at least two rounds of lovemaking, she wasn't about to complain.

As enjoyable as lying in bed was, she had work to do. Today she wanted to finish the painting of Charles, Jacques, and Daniel that Jacques had asked her to paint weeks ago. He was going to present it to Charles at the festival.

Then there were a few last-minute details for tomorrow's event to tidy up. Jacques had insisted on hiring someone to deal with problems on the day so Maya could enjoy the party. She'd spent two days with the event planner and felt confident the woman could handle any eventualities even better than Maya could. Michelle would be attending and available to help as well.

Jacques had asked her several times about what she was going to wear, even offering to take her to Paris. But she wanted it to be a secret, a surprise. She wiggled away from him, trying not to wake him, but he stirred at the loss of her body heat.

"Where are you going? It's barely dawn." His sexy morning voice nearly made her crawl back against him.

"I've got work to do. We aren't all billionaire *comtes*-in-waiting who can laze in bed all day."

He sat up, the sheet dropping to his waist and exposing his naked chest. She licked her lips, and a come-here smile pulled his mouth upward. God, that smile could melt concrete. "You keep harping on about my title. I think you want one of your own." He said it teasingly, but his eyes had suddenly turned serious.

She laughed, but there was an edge of nervousness in it. "Can you imagine me with a title? Maya, the inked countess."

"Having tattoos doesn't disqualify you from being a countess. Especially when the count able to confer the title is very fond of them."

She completely ignored the veiled implication, because it was just too mind-blowing to contemplate at that early hour. "If you're so fond of tattoos, why don't you have one?"

"Maybe I'll get one. Maybe I'll have the name *Maya* tattooed over my heart."

"That will seriously limit your dating pool in the future."

Alexia Adams

"I'm afraid you've already done that. I've found I'm only drawn to auburn-haired, amber-eyed, Canadian artists with cupcake tattoos on their left hip bone."

"Well, that does reduce your options." And it increased her heart rate. What was he saying?

"Yes, it is rather restricting. But the heart wants what it wants."

It was too intense. She needed a strategic retreat. "If you start singing that Selena Gomez song, I'm going to video it and put it up on YouTube."

Jacques heaved a pretend sigh, throwing his hands in the air. "What's a man to do? He tries to be romantic and woo his woman, and he gets threatened with Internet infamy." His crushed expression made her return to the bed.

"You don't need to woo me. I'm already under your spell."

"Right this minute I wish you were under my body."

He kissed her, his lips tempting her to lose herself in the ecstasy he so easily engulfed her in. But if the painting was going to be dry enough to present to Charles at the party tomorrow night, she was already cutting it close.

"I've got to go. If I'm not back by six, send someone to get me."

After another enthusiastic kiss, Jacques finally released her. Yup, a girl could get used to such a life.

***

Maya stood back and stared at the painting. It was

143

good. She'd spent two days just deciding what expression to put on their faces. Charles had been easy. She'd painted the twinkle in his eyes and the welcoming smile on his lips. Daniel she'd finally put in race mode, his competitiveness, focus, and determination clearly shown on his face. It was Jacques she'd spent the longest contemplating. She wanted to paint him as she'd wistfully drawn him the day he'd fallen asleep after his migraine—with love and hope in his eyes. Or she could capture him as he was now, satiated and relaxed, on the verge of happiness. But she didn't know if it would last. Yes, he'd hinted about the future, even more so this morning. But there was still one huge obstacle. The price on her head. So she'd painted him as she'd first seen him—powerful, determined, and lonely.

She stretched out a kink in her back then glanced at the clock. She had just enough time to get back to the chateau, shower, and dress before Jacques would be finished with his meeting. If she wasn't ready by the time he made his way upstairs, he'd join her in the shower and then they'd be late for dinner. Again. She'd moved the painting to the cottage so it would be a surprise for Charles—and so it would prevent Jacques from distracting her every fifteen minutes.

Getting dressed up for dinner was one custom she'd never thought she'd like. But it made each meal an occasion. A time to step away from the day, chill out, and enjoy the fine food and even better company. It didn't hurt that she got to wear her sexy dresses, and she and Jacques would touch each other under the table so that by the time Charles said goodnight, they barely made it upstairs before ripping each other's clothes off. She'd had more than one seam to repair the following day. Good thing Marie Dubois claimed to love sewing.

Quickly cleaning her brushes, Maya was about to lock up the cottage when she heard her cell phone ring. *God no, not now.* She dug it out of the basket where she'd hidden it and answered.

"You okay?" Her brother's strong Canadian accent came over loud and clear. She'd been speaking French for so long now, it took a few seconds for her brain to switch back to English.

"Of course," she replied. "What's up?"

"I've been calling this number for days and you haven't answered. I was scared something had happened to you."

"Oh, sorry to have worried you. I've been busy." *Living it up with the lord of the manor.*

"Maya, the cops have been by again."

"God, Sean, I'm sorry. Is it making life difficult for you? You're not about to lose your job, are you?"

"No, actually, it's helping with my street cred. There's a warrant out for your arrest."

"What? I haven't done anything. I've been out of the country for the past two months, for God's sake."

"I told you they issued a subpoena for you to attend court and testify. They've tracked your passport to France. And they've been asking about Gran-Gran and whether we still have family there. It may not be long before they find you. Be careful, okay? And for my sake, would you please call me once a week so I know you're safe?"

"Yeah, sure."

"I love you, Maya. You're a massive pain in the

ass, but I don't want anything to happen to you."

"Thanks. I love you, too."

She canceled the call and whirled around at the indrawn breath she heard. Jacques had the same expression on his face that she'd painted. Nailed it. It was a hollow victory.

"Who do you love, Maya?" His voice was harsh, his hands clenched at his sides.

You. Except now probably wasn't the time to admit it. "My brother, Sean. Remember, I told you about him. He's a teacher, helps kids in trouble."

"You also told me you didn't have a phone." He relaxed a fraction, his hands no longer fisted.

"Well, I have one for emergencies. But I never use it. I certainly don't text while in bed with you." She approached him, her eyes searching his.

"Is there something you aren't telling me, Maya? Everything okay back home? That seemed very tense for a random conversation with your brother."

"No, it's all good. Sean was just telling me off for not calling him regularly. He was worried when he didn't hear from me in the past few weeks."

She should tell him. Except she'd have to tell him everything. Jacques hated risks he couldn't control, and being with her was the greatest risk of all. Confessing now would be messy and probably end their relationship. And she didn't want that the day before the festival. She'd tell him right after. Another twenty-four hours couldn't hurt. Could it?

Chapter 16

"*Merde.*"

She didn't hear Jacques swear often. So she looked up from the list she'd been checking. He strode across the hallway, his body vibrating with anger.

"What's wrong?" She dropped the clipboard onto a nearby table. His mouth had hardened to a tight line, and a muscle in his jaw pulsed. Her heart rate accelerated. Had he found out she was wanted by both the RCMP and Big Tony?

"My mother," he answered.

Bullet dodged. This time. Although from his expression, he was about as excited to hear from his mother as to be told he needed a root canal. "Oh, that answers nothing." She caressed his cheek and he covered her hand with his before sliding it across and kissing her palm. If her knees went a bit weak, it was just because she'd been standing too long.

"My mother has heard about the festival. She called to say she will attend and will require four bedrooms for her entourage, as she doesn't wish to return to Paris if the party goes late."

"Would you call that presumptuous or self-assured?" she teased. Except he wasn't laughing.

"She treats this like it's still her house. She left. Left me. Left Daniel. She didn't come back for birthdays or Christmas or anything. What right does she have to come to our party?" A thrill raced through

147

her when he said "our party."

"Well, we have two choices. We can get four bedrooms ready, greet your mother when she arrives, and then ignore her for the evening as we enjoy ourselves. Then tomorrow we can stay in bed until she leaves, and aside from ten minutes when she first gets here, you never have to talk with her."

"Tempting. And option two?"

"You tell your mother she's not welcome and spend the entire festival expecting her to show up and make a scene. When she does arrive uninvited, wait half an hour for the police to get here and escort her off the premises. And tomorrow morning, rather than make love to me, make an application for a restraining order to stop her from ever setting foot on your property again."

He stared into her eyes, but she already knew his decision. He kissed her, his lips lingering on hers. "Promise we can spend tomorrow in bed until she departs?"

"We can make so much noise, your mother will leave early just to get some peace and quiet."

"You present a compelling argument. I'll tell Marie to get the rooms ready."

He kissed Maya briefly then walked towards the ballroom where the housekeeper was assisting with the setup for the party. With so much to do, getting four bedrooms ready for unexpected guests wasn't going to be easy. Maya would help. She knew the perfect bedspread for Jacques's mother's room.

"Oh, Jacques…" He turned back. "My dress isn't the only surprise. I bought something to wear after everyone leaves. For your eyes only, if you know what I mean."

His sexy grin returned. "That thought is going to keep me going through whatever happens tonight."

As she fidgeted beside Jacques four hours later, she wished she had a fast-forward button so she could be modeling her new negligee for him. Instead, she was standing on the top step as six white Rolls Royces pulled up in front of the chateau. Jacques grabbed her hand and squeezed it lightly. Based on Jacques's reaction to news of his mother's arrival, she didn't need to worry about impressing the matron. She had half a mind to tell the woman off for abandoning her children. She didn't want to reopen old wounds, though. For Jacques's sake, she'd keep her peace.

Grace and serenity, Maya. You can do it.

A woman in her late fifties stepped from the back of the first car after the chauffeur opened the door. She was immaculately dressed, head to toe in Chanel. Her dark hair was swept up in an elegant chignon, and oversized sunglasses hid her eyes. Other people began spilling from the cars. Even if they were couples, the new arrivals would need way more than four bedrooms. Maya gritted her teeth. Maybe they weren't all staying.

"Jacques!" The woman waved and hurried over to them as though they were on the best of terms. Jacques's hand moved from Maya's to around her waist, pulling her tightly against his side.

"*Maman*." There was no warmth in his greeting, and if Maya hadn't been watching very carefully, she might have missed the slight hesitation in his mother's step.

The Vintner and The Vixen

"Are you going to introduce me, *mon cher*?"

"Maya, this is my mother, Audette Michaud Martin. *Maman*, this is Maya Tessier." No explanation about her role in his life. But his arm around her and the way his voice softened on her name spoke volumes. Maya's chest swelled. It was going to be okay.

The rest of the group joined them on the step, and, as she expected, Jacques's mother began to play hostess as though she still lived here. Four more rooms were needed, and Maya left to help get them ready. It had been decades since so many people stayed at the house, and although the rooms were kept moderately clean, they still needed airing, the bed sheets needed freshening, and towels and toiletries had to be found. Just what the household needed on the busiest day of the year. She was beginning to think that option two, sending Jacques's mother packing, might have been the better choice.

As a result, Maya was an hour late to the winery and so frazzled that she almost missed the symbolic first crush of the grapes. This was the family event, whereas the party tonight was adults only. Six small children from the village were vigorously stomping on the grapes in a big wooden vat. Shrieks of laughter filled the air and almost everyone in attendance had their phones or cameras out, filming the fun.

Outside, local businesses had set up stalls promoting their wares or services. There were free party games and a dunk tank. Clowns and mascots dressed as clusters of grapes circulated, handing out candy and small presents. From the smiles on everyone's faces, it was a roaring success.

So why did she feel like the bouncy castle with its blower turned off?

Jacques was busy having his photo taken with the local dignitaries, so she steered well clear of him. At least there wouldn't be press at the party that night, so she would likely be safe. She found a quiet corner, took a deep breath, and repeated Gran-Gran's mantra. When that didn't work, she tried *suck it up, buttercup*.

Jacques's mother was making her presence felt at every opportunity, her entourage following her around as though she were royalty.

"She's a piece of work, isn't she?"

Maya turned to find Daniel leaning against the wall behind her.

"When did you get here?" She was so glad to see a friendly face that she hugged him.

"Just after you. Sorry I'm late. Although I'm not sorry I missed the circus at the house. *Maman* likes nothing better than to make everyone dance around her."

"Well, I plan to save my dancing for later. Have you seen Charles? I can't find him anywhere." She scanned the group again but couldn't spot him.

"He said he'd give this bit a miss. He's saving his strength for tonight."

"He's all right, isn't he? I know that at his age, one day they can be fine and the next struggling for breath in hospital." Her great-grandmother's quick demise still plagued her. Especially since the catalyst for Gran-Gran's sudden ill health had been Maya's arrest.

"He's fine. I think he'd just rather avoid

Maman."

"Wouldn't we all."

Daniel laughed. "You fit right in, Maya. I'm so glad you and Jacques got together." With that pronouncement he pushed away from the wall and disappeared into the crowd.

Would he feel the same after she told Jacques what was waiting for her back in Canada? All the excitement of the day fizzled away.

It was the beginning of the end.

***

Jacques scanned the crowd for Maya. He wanted her at his side. *Maudit*, he wanted her upstairs in his bed, but he'd settle for beside him. For now. He'd barely caught a glimpse of her at the winery, and she'd come back on her motorbike before the rest of them, so he hadn't even had a chance to tell her how fabulous the festival was.

All the guests were in the foyer, waiting for him to open the doors to the ballroom so the party could begin. But he wasn't starting without her.

"Daniel, have you seen Maya?" His brother was hanging in the shadows, avoiding their mother.

"Last saw her with Grand-Papa in the *petit salon*."

"Thanks." Jacques hurried to the room at the back of the house, the one where they met before dinner. He opened the door just as Maya was handing a glass of water to his grandfather.

Jacques's heart stopped. Then began beating out of control. Maya was so beautiful, he stood for a full minute just staring at her. Her auburn hair was pulled up, but a few tendrils caressed her cheeks. Her amber eyes looked huge with the way she'd applied her makeup. And the dress. *Dieu*, the dress. The dark blue satin hugged her curves and then fell in folds to the ground. Her creamy skin looked almost ethereal against the dark color. Maybe he should shut the door and the three of them could spend a quiet evening together.

Except Maya had worked hard to make this event function smoothly. And he had a surprise for her.

"You look stunning, Maya."

"She's as beautiful as Yvette," Grand-Papa said, his voice scratchy.

A soft pink tinged her cheeks as she kissed his grandfather on the cheek. The telltale blush was as indicative of her nerves as a shaking hand. Her bold confidence needed a kick start.

She checked her watch. "What are you doing here? You're supposed to open the ballroom doors and invite everyone in."

"I'm waiting for you. And pissing off my mother by making her stand in the hallway."

Maya sighed. "The sooner we get this started, the sooner it will be over." Her excitement for the festival seemed to have gone. After all the work she'd done, he wasn't about to let his mother ruin the day.

"I have a surprise, and I want you to be the first to see it."

"Really?" Her eyes widened and a small smile lifted her lips.

"Yes. Come on. The three of us are going to start this party, and it'll be the best harvest festival this house has seen in decades."

"Since there hasn't been a festival in decades, that's not a great achievement. But I won't argue," she muttered.

He took his grandfather's arm and the three of them made their way back to the hallway and up four of the stairs so they could be seen by all. He maneuvered them so Maya stood on his right and his grandfather on his left.

"Ladies and gentlemen, welcome to Chateau de Vendee's first harvest festival of the twenty-first century. Such an event would not have been possible without the hard work and creativity of the woman beside me, Maya Tessier." Jacques paused for the applause and nodded at Daniel. "Even though Maya has been with us a short time, she has become an integral part of the de Launay family. And knowing us so well, I asked her to paint something for my grandfather."

Daniel climbed the stairs to bring them the canvas Maya had painted. With a flourish he pulled off the loose sheet and showed it first to Grand-Papa and then to the audience. Another long round of applause broke out. A tear trickled down his grandfather's face as he thanked Maya for the beautiful painting. She bent down and kissed his cheek, thanking him for letting her into his life.

Maya was in all their lives, Jacques's especially. Their truce agreement specifically precluded love, but that didn't mean it hadn't happened. She now owned more than the cottage and land; she'd taken his heart, something that couldn't be returned with a sale agreement. Right this second, he'd rip up the maintenance invoice and give it all to her if she'd say she loved him in return. He now knew exactly how his grandfather had felt all those years ago when he'd gifted the property to the woman he loved. It was no longer a weakness in Jacques's eyes. It showed the depth of his devotion. *Maudit*, when the de Launays loved, they didn't do it by half measures.

He had to swallow before he could speak. "The painting will be on display in the ballroom as well as another surprise." He put his arm around Maya and led her down the stairs, along the hall to the ballroom doors. The crowd followed behind, excitedly speculating about the next reveal.

He flung open the double doors and heard Maya's gasp. Her sculpture stood in the center of the room, raised on a dais, directly below the chandelier, which flooded the piece with light.

"Why? How?" She simply stared as if she'd never seen it before.

"This morning the rental company broke the statue you had originally intended to be the centerpiece. The event planner couldn't find you because you were making beds upstairs. So I had your piece moved in. I wanted to show everyone what an amazing artist you are."

"Thank you." She squeezed his hand and stood on tiptoe to whisper in his ear. "I hope you like my surprise tonight as much."

And Maya was back.

The crowd surged around them, and the next couple of hours were spent conversing with people he hadn't seen in a long time—local villagers he'd gone to school with, people who had worked on the grape harvest, dignitaries, and executives from the wine industry. Maya stood at his side and spoke with each one as if she'd known them for years herself. He couldn't have asked for a better companion. She even had the chair of the Heritage Society eating out of her hand, complimenting her on the new decor as if it were her house and not his. Not that he minded. If they could make this relationship work, she'd truly become his partner, helping him run the estate and sharing his responsibilities. It seemed almost easier to breathe.

Everyone commented on the beauty and detail of Maya's art. Several even offered to purchase the statue. Maya looked torn about selling her work, and he wasn't about to let it go. Not when it meant so much to him personally. "I'm sorry, the piece is already sold," he told one persistent person.

"You sold my work without talking to me?" Maya asked when they had two seconds alone. The fire in her eyes warned him to tread carefully.

"I want it. I'll pay double what anyone else offers, or you can name your price."

She smiled and he caught his breath. Would he ever get used to her effect on him? "We can negotiate a price tonight, when we're alone." The event planner signaled to her from across the room. "Excuse me. I need to check on something, I'll be right back."

"Want company?" His hand had more than once itched to stray from her bare back to the curve of her ass so perfectly displayed in navy satin.

He got another of her sexy smiles, and his pants became too tight. "Later. Save a dance for me."

The band had begun to play, and people were

Alexia Adams

dancing at the end of the ballroom. His gaze was firmly fixed on Maya's backside as she strode toward the door.

"Really, Jacques," *Maman* said as she approached, sipping a glass of sparkling wine. "Can you not be a bit more discreet? Parading your lover so blatantly in public is beneath someone of your social position."

"We're not in public. This is my home. And Maya is more than my lover." *So much more.* "Anyway, I no longer take advice from you, especially about relationships. Speaking of which, where is your husband?"

"In bed with some other woman, knowing him."

He wasn't rising to the bait. *Maman* was hardly one to complain about marital fidelity, given Daniel's birth while she was still legally married to Jacques's father. Then as soon as she'd married Thierry Martin, her sons had been inconvenient to her new life and they'd both been left to live with Grand-Papa. "Why are you here?"

"To see my sons."

"Cut the crap. We've been here for years, and you've never come before."

She shrugged, clearly not caring that he'd seen through her lie. "Thierry wants a divorce. And due to the prenuptial agreement, I will have only a fraction of my current income."

"You want money." She nodded. "I owe you nothing. I suggest you start shopping for husband number three," he said.

"Oh, I already have. Pierre is away on business at the moment, but he wants to meet you. He has this

157

company. It's failing at the moment, but with the right injection of capital…"

Maman would never change. She would never say, "It's nice to see you happy for once, Jacques." He gritted his teeth. "Enough. I'm not discussing this with you now. I need to check on Grand-Papa, make sure he's okay."

He walked away without looking back.

Grand-Papa was talking with some old friends and waved at Jacques. At least someone was enjoying the party.

When Maya hadn't returned twenty minutes later, he went looking for her. Maybe she needed a minute alone and had escaped to the *petit salon*. Discreet security personnel were stationed throughout the house, keeping guests away from the family areas, the *petit salon* being one of them. As he approached he heard her talking. Damn, she wasn't alone. He'd been hoping for a taster of tonight's private activities.

"You think you're going to be his second wife, don't you?" The shrillness in his mother's tone reminded him of the fight his parents had before *Maman* left—the accusations of infidelity, the hateful words she'd screamed as she realized she'd lost it all. Whatever game she was playing now, Maya obviously wasn't as easy to intimidate as *Maman* had expected.

"Jacques and I haven't discussed marriage," Maya replied calmly. "But if we did, I can tell you this: I have no intention of being his second wife."

His blood froze.

Chapter 17

It was two in the morning before the last guests left and those who were staying overnight were shown to their rooms. Maya was exhausted, but an electric energy pulsed through her body. After the encounter with Jacques's mother in the sitting room, he'd appeared and whisked her away. But he was different, more remote. His kisses had been hard, and he'd held her a little too tightly as they danced. Had she overstepped the bounds somewhere? Sure, she'd pretended in her own mind that she was his wife; she'd just wanted to see what it would feel like to be his partner in life. But he hadn't worked out her game, had he?

Up in their bedroom, he poured himself a cognac and leaned against the doorframe as she removed her jewelry in the walk-in closet they now shared.

"What's wrong? Did I do something to upset you?" she asked as he continued to stare.

"What did you mean when you told my mother you'd never be my second wife?"

Because I want to be your last wife. Except she couldn't tell him that. She couldn't say she loved him or ask him to say it to her. There was still so much he didn't know, and she didn't want him to say things he'd regret when he found out. Tomorrow, after his mother left, she'd tell him everything. If he didn't take the news well, she wasn't going to give Audette Michaud the satisfaction of hearing them break up.

Or seeing her cry. This had the potential to rip her heart to shreds.

To hide her insecurity, she went on the offensive. "God, next time I make an agreement with you I'm going to put it in writing. No love, remember? It was the first stipulation, I recall. I know you think love shouldn't be a part of marriage, but I do. I won't marry a man I don't love. Or one who doesn't love me. So that kind of disqualifies me from becoming your second, third, or fourth wife. Besides, I wasn't going to play whatever mind games your mother had planned."

He slung back his drink, put the glass on the dresser, and then advanced on her. Their gazes met in the full-length mirror. "I remember exactly what we agreed. But there are only five days left in our initial term. And I will be dictating the articles this time."

She caught her breath at the intensity in his eyes. Was he upset because he didn't think she wanted him? That was easily fixed. "Will you be wearing a negligee to negotiate? Because I've got one I haven't worn yet. I could give it to you."

The corner of his mouth twitched up. "No. I have my own ways to get what I want. Five days, Maya. You'd better think long and hard about what you want. Because this will be our last agreement."

That wasn't difficult. She wanted him. She wanted his love. Those two things were non-negotiable; everything else was filler. "I'd better make full use of the time I have left while the terms are in my favor. Can you help me with the zipper on my dress? It's a bit stiff and hard to manage on my own."

"You could have asked me to help when you put on the dress." But instead of undoing the fastener, he pulled her against him, her back to his chest. His lips moved from her ear down her neck to her shoulder, one hand cupping her breast, the other across her stomach.

"Yeah, right. For you zippers only go in one direction—down." He alternated between nipping the cord of her neck with his teeth and soothing the sting with his tongue. The hand at her breast had slipped inside the fabric and toyed with her nipple. Seriously, she was about to ignite. If he didn't get this damn dress off her soon, she'd set it on fire.

His lips moved to her ear. "It is more enjoyable helping you out of your clothes. This is a beautiful gown, though. Where'd you get it?"

"It was my Gran-Gran's. She wore it the night she got engaged to your grandfather."

His head lifted at that, and he scrutinized her reflection again. "Did Grand-Papa recognize it?"

"Yes. He said he was glad to see it again on someone he loved."

An odd light shone in Jacques's eyes. "We'd better be careful with it, then. You never know when you might want to wear it again." He undid the dress just enough to ease the fabric off her shoulders and bare her breasts. Both his hands were fondling her now, and she locked her knees to remain upright. She let out a low moan, and he slid the fabric from her arms. Then he looped her arms around the back of his neck, unzipping the rest of the dress and shoving it off her hips. She stood in front of the mirror, wearing only her heels and a lacy thong. The underwear lasted about two seconds before he tore them from her body. He was still fully dressed, including his tie and suit jacket.

"I feel a bit disadvantaged here," she said.

"That's odd, because from where I'm standing, you're the one in control. I couldn't move from you if I wanted. Have you ever watched yourself orgasm? It's a beautiful sight." Their gazes were still locked in the mirror. One of his hands was between her thighs, the other tormenting her breasts. Her skin was pink all over and her breathing rapid.

"No, I haven't." She gasped as his fingers worked their magic. Mesmerized, she watched his hands on her body; the combined sensory impact of sight and touch heightened the sensations. She came with such intensity that everything went black for a moment.

When she finally stopped quivering, he turned her to face him. "Be prepared. When we renegotiate, I'm going to demand exclusivity. You are mine, Maya, whether you want to admit it yet or not."

She rested her forehead against his neck. "That clause works both ways."

"I'm aware of that. Now, about your new negligee…"

***

Jacques woke with a Maya hangover. Which was the best kind. It came with no headache or nausea, just a huge smile and an unwillingness to ever leave the bed. The night before had been spectacular. He didn't know whether it was finally admitting to himself that

162

he loved her, or the overwhelming suspicion that she felt the same, but even the sex had seemed different. It was just as intense and passionate, but now it was enhanced by an emotional connection and sense of belonging that hadn't been there before. *Dieu*, if he didn't regain control, any second now he'd start singing some sappy love song. Then Maya would wake up and make some smart-ass comment, and he'd laugh. Life with her would not be dull.

Her promise of getting their unwelcome guests to leave by disturbing their peace had also been filled. He'd loved her over and over until neither of them could move. At one point, as dawn was breaking, he'd heard the sound of a bedroom door being slammed somewhere down the corridor.

He sat up so he could see her better. Her hair was spread across the pillow, her hand tucked under her cheek. She looked so peaceful, so beautiful, he didn't have the heart to wake her, even though his cock was stirring to life. The creaminess of her shoulder begged for his kisses; he wanted to trail them down her arm and then up her torso until he took one taut nipple into his mouth and let his tongue drive her to a climax. She had the most sensitive breasts, full and firm—he could spend hours tasting them. And he had.

But his goal this morning was to get rid of his mother so Maya didn't have to deal with her. And that would require a delay in his fantasy. *Tant pis.* Pity. There was always tonight. Or perhaps a little pre-dinner appetizer.

He eased out of bed, had a quick shower, and dressed. Maya didn't even stir as he searched the room for his phone.

The dining room and *petit salon* were both deserted, even though it was almost ten o'clock. Surely someone would be up by now.

"Good night?" Daniel asked when Jacques finally found him in the library.

"Fantastic. Yours?"

"Lonely."

"I don't imagine that will last for long," Jacques said.

"I don't know. I'm tiring of having a different woman every night. Seeing how happy you are with Maya makes me think I'm doing it all wrong."

"I'm sure it's just a phase."

Daniel shrugged. "Probably."

"Have you seen Grand-Papa this morning? He's usually reading the paper in the *petit salon* by now."

"Actually, I haven't. Maybe he's just sleeping late."

Jacques checked his watch. It was ten thirty. He couldn't remember a time when his grandfather wasn't up by nine, no matter how late the night.

"I think we should check on him. The festival was rather eventful." And seeing Maya in Yvette's dress had to have brought back memories, both good and bad.

They wandered down to the wing where Grand-Papa had his rooms. It was far from the festivities of the party, and he'd said good night to him and Maya at eleven, so it wasn't as if he'd been up all night.

Jacques knocked softly on the door, then a little harder when it went unanswered. A chill swept down his spine as he caught Daniel's eye. His brother looked as concerned as he was. His hand shook slightly as he turned the handle. They had to walk through a small sitting room before they came to Grand-Papa's actual bedroom. There was no light coming from under the door, so the curtains were still drawn. Jacques's heart rate quickened, a sickening dread making his stomach churn. *Dieu*, not today.

He didn't bother to knock this time, easing the door open as quietly as possible. From the faint light through a crack in the curtain they could make out Grand-Papa laying on his bed, not moving. They both rushed to the side. Daniel had his phone in hand, ready to call for help.

If they weren't too late.

"He's still breathing," Jacques said, having put his ear against his grandfather's chest. "And his heart is beating, but it's very faint and slow."

"Grand-Papa, wake up," Daniel said gently.

But there was no movement on the bed. Jacques touched his grandfather's face, and still he didn't move.

"Call an ambulance," Jacques instructed.

A heavy weight settled on his chest, making it difficult to drag in a lungful of air. Why was life so goddamned determined to see him miserable?

"I'll stay with him. You go get Maya," Daniel said.

Jacques didn't question him and raced from the room. He needed her. Desperately.

Chapter 18

The next two hours were the longest of Jacques's life. The ambulance came and took his grandfather to the hospital. Grand-Papa regained consciousness briefly before slipping back into oblivion.

They sat in the hospital waiting room. Maya's creamy skin was ashen, and she'd chewed at least three nails down to the quick. He shouldn't have brought her. Would she try to avoid further heartache by distancing herself from Grand-Papa and him?

"I'm sorry, I should have thought. This must bring back bad memories. I can get a car to take you back to the chateau," he offered as she wiped another tear from the corner of her eye.

"No. I'm fine. Well, not fine, but I want to be here. When Gran-Gran passed, I was alone. My grandmother didn't have a phone so I couldn't call her, and my mom couldn't afford to fly out. It was just me. I need to be here for you and Daniel." She took his hand in hers. Of all their recent intimacy, this was the most touching. It wasn't lust; it was partnership.

Daniel paced the corridor—restless, alone.

"Your being here means a lot to me, to us, and I'm sure Grand-Papa will be happy to see you as well." Jacques had to keep optimistic.

"Monsieur de Launay?" A doctor approached, his face devoid of emotion. Maya squeezed Jacques's hand tighter, and he could tell she was holding her breath.

"Yes?" He stood, bracing himself for bad news.

"We've stabilized your grandfather. It was a combination of his heart rate being too low and his blood sugar being too high. If you hadn't brought him in when you did, it could have been much worse. We'll keep him here for a few days, change some of his medicines, and make sure everything else is in order. But he's a strong man, and I'm sure he'll be home again before midweek."

Relief weakened his knees and Jacques fell back into his chair. Maya released his hand and rubbed his back.

Her voice wobbled as she said, "Can we see him now?"

"As long as you keep it brief," the doctor replied.

They followed the white-coated physician down the hallway and into a private room. Grand-Papa lay with the head of the bed elevated; he was hooked up to various machines, a reassuring beep coming steadily from one of them. His eyes were open, and he smiled as they entered. Maya let go of Jacques's hand and raced to his grandfather's bedside. She wasn't even related, had only met the man two months before, and still she cared for him like he was her own grandfather. Clarisse had never shown any affection for the old man—she barely even spoke with him, despite the fact that they shared a house for three years. If Jacques had needed any further proof that Maya was the woman for him, he now had it.

"Charles, you gave us such a scare. Or was this all an elaborate ploy to hang out with some beautiful nurses?" Maya planted a kiss on his grandfather's cheek before sitting on the edge of the bed.

"Ha, you caught on. Sorry to have worried you. I guess in all the excitement I forgot to take my medicines yesterday," Grand-Papa said. "And, pretty nurses aside, how soon can I go home?"

"In a few days," Jacques replied. "They want to run some tests on you first."

They stayed a few more minutes, but it was obvious even that small conversation had tired his grandfather. They left with a promise to return later in the afternoon.

As Daniel drove them back to the chateau, Jacques sat in the backseat. He tried to hold Maya's hand, but she pulled away and stared out the window. From the number of tissues she'd pulled out of her bag, the tears were flowing like the Seine. Was this all about his grandfather? Or was something else bothering her? She'd been on edge for the past couple of days, but he'd put it down to stress over the festival.

"Grand-Papa's going to be fine," he said.

A loud snuffle preceded her cracked voice. "I can't do this again. I can't live like this."

The same chill that had run down his spine when he'd discovered his grandfather unconscious swept through him again.

***

Maya stared at the mural on the ceiling in the chateau's hallway, blinking back more tears. Seeing Charles in hospital, hooked up to all those machines, reminded her so much of Gran-Gran that she'd barely

168

kept it together.

The shock of Maya's arrest had led to her great-grandmother's death. She couldn't let Charles pay the price as well. There was no other way; she'd have to leave before that could happen. Jacques would never forgive her if he knew the risk she was taking with all of their lives. Pain radiated from her chest, numbing her limbs.

Jacques was explaining to the housekeeper about his grandfather's condition, but he kept his gaze on Maya. He'd been so stoic, so concerned about Charles—it was a replica of what she'd felt for Gran-Gran. Having now met his mother, she could understand his devotion to his grandfather, the only adult who had loved him unconditionally through his life. She needed to support and comfort him, not dump her worries on him the second they returned from the hospital. Besides, she was way too emotional to shovel up the shit from her past now.

"I wasn't sure when you would be back, so I prepared a cold lunch," the housekeeper told Jacques. "I can bring it to the dining room if you wish."

"Maya, are you hungry?"

"Yes." The word came out a bare whisper. She really needed to get herself under control.

"And your mother is still here. She's in the *petit salon*. Her friends have departed," Marie said before turning to leave.

"*Dieu*, I thought she'd have gone by now as well. Let's eat first. I can't face my mother on an empty stomach," Jacques said. He took Maya's hand and led her to the dining room. His strong fingers laced with hers felt too good to pull away.

"Maybe she stayed to find out about your grandfather," she suggested.

"Unlikely. She was never fond of Grand-Papa. After we eat, why don't you go up to the room and have a nap? Then I can get rid of *Maman* and join you."

She was exhausted. And it would be easier to explain why she had to leave if her brain wasn't so muddled.

After a quiet lunch that she hoped Jacques put down to her worry over Charles, they parted at the door to the sitting room. His face was grim and a muscle pulsed in his jaw. She squeezed his hand in silent support before she climbed the stairs.

Walking through the bedroom to the closet, she pulled out her suitcase. Then the enormity of what she had to do hit her like a bus, and she pushed it back into place, resting her forehead on the wall. There was no way she'd be able to tell Jacques with grace and serenity. *Oh, Gran-Gran, how did you do this? How did you rip out your heart and still live?*

Back in the bedroom she stripped down to her underwear and crawled under the covers. Just a few minutes…

A faint pink light shone through a crack between the curtains when Maya woke. It took her a couple of moments to remember where she was and what day it was. Jacques wasn't at her back, and, rolling over, she discovered he wasn't even in bed.

"Has anyone told you how beautiful you are when you sleep?" Jacques's deep voice came to her from across the room. He had his laptop set up on the table where they'd had breakfast a few times.

"I'd rather be told I'm beautiful when I'm awake," she replied, sitting up.

"You are lethal when you're awake." As far as compliments went, that one was open to interpretation. "You walk into a room and I can barely remember to breathe." Much better.

"What time is it?" *Time to rip my life to shreds?*

"Nearly eight."

"Eight? Why didn't you wake me?" She flung back the covers and hunted around for her clothes. "We were supposed to return to visit your grandfather in hospital this afternoon." *And then I was going to tell you I'm leaving.*

Jacques rose and wrapped his arms around her. "I called the hospital, and they said Grand-Papa was sleeping so not to come until tomorrow morning. They'll telephone me immediately if there's any change in his situation. Daniel has gone back to Paris, taking my mother with him. So there's only us. And you obviously needed the rest. But I couldn't bear to be away from you, so I brought my laptop up and worked from here. Do you know you giggle in your sleep? For a bad, tattooed biker girl, you certainly are cute."

She raised her gaze to his, memorizing the look in his eyes. "For a cold, ruthless billionaire, you certainly talk sweet."

His lips descended and the kiss they shared was so full of promise Maya didn't want it to end. Jacques unhooked her bra and his hand came around to cup her breast, the rough pad of his thumb circling her nipple. Passion flared, and she pulled his hips closer to grind against his growing erection. He groaned and his lips left hers to trail down her throat. *One last time before I go.*

His phone rang.

"I'd better get that; it could be the hospital," he said.

As he released her, a draft of cool air blew across her hot skin, making her shiver. She refastened her bra and reached for her wrap as Jacques answered the phone.

"What? How the hell did that happen?"

She froze. He must have noticed the blood drain from her face because he pulled the phone away from his mouth for a second. "It's Daniel, not the hospital."

Relieved that his grandfather appeared, at least for the moment, to be okay, she relaxed for a second—only to seize up at his next words.

"That is a blatant invasion of our privacy. She'll never set foot on this property again." Daniel was speaking on the other end, but she couldn't hear him. "Okay. Thanks for calling. Yeah, I'll keep you up to date on Grand-Papa's condition. Bye, Daniel."

Jacques put his phone down, but rather than resume their embrace, he strode over to his laptop. Maya joined him.

"What's happened?"

"Mother." He opened a search engine and began typing.

"Again, not so helpful. What did she want? Why did she stay when the rest of her friends left?"

"She wants money. Her marriage is ending and her current lover has liquidity issues, so she needs something to live on. I gave her a million euros and told her that was all she was ever going to get. Had I known she'd pulled this stunt, I wouldn't have given her a single cent."

Maya's heart thudded in her chest. "What's she done?" But the answer was staring her in the face. On Jacques's laptop screen was a photo of her and Jacques at the party last night. Underneath was the caption: Next Comte de Vendee, Jacques de Launay, captivated by unknown Canadian artist Maya Tessier.

Her blood ran cold and she started to shake all over. She clutched the edge of the table to keep upright.

"Daniel says it's all over the Internet. One of *Maman*'s entourage was a journalist for one of the trashy celebrity magazines. He even caught us kissing in the hallway." Jacques scrolled down a few more photos while Maya sank into the chair. He grabbed his cell phone from the table and called another number.

He barely gave the other person a second to answer the phone before he began to bark orders while he paced. "I want a takedown notice issued immediately. I want all photos and any mention of me or Maya off the Internet by morning. Then sue the bastards for enough to put them out of business permanently." A pause. "No, they were taken on private property, within my house, and they didn't have my agreement." Another pause. "He came with my mother. I did not invite him." A longer pause this time, and Jacques scraped a hand through his hair. "I don't give a shit how you do it. Hire a hacker for all I care. Get the goddamned photos off the Internet. And if they appear in print, heads will roll. I don't want my relationship with Maya publicized. And I sure as hell don't want them to dredge up Clarisse's death again."

The poor person on the other end of the call was trying to calm Jacques, but he wasn't having it. "If they're not off by 9:00 a.m. tomorrow, then buy the whole damn company and shut them down. Fire every single employee. I don't care what it costs."

He canceled the call and tossed his phone back on the table. He scrubbed his face with both hands. Then he turned to her.

"Don't think this is because I'm embarrassed to be seen with you. But after Clarisse's death, there was a lot of very nasty press, including rumors that I had been unfaithful and abused her. I had to sue several publications, and even though I was exonerated in court, it took a toll on me, Grand-Papa, Daniel, and even my businesses. I won't allow anyone to profit from my personal life."

If only he knew how this was about to blow up.

She went over to him, put her hands on his face, stood on tiptoe, and kissed him. "I understand. I have something—"

There was a frantic pounding on the bedroom door. Jacques automatically turned and pushed her behind him to protect her.

"Monsieur Jacques, the police are here. The house is surrounded. They are demanding to see Mademoiselle Maya." The frantic voice of the butler came through the paneled door. "They say if she is not down in two minutes, they will come up."

Jacques turned to her, his face white.

"Maya?"

Chapter 19

Maya grabbed her clothes off the chair and pulled them on as fast as possible. She'd barely done up her jeans when she heard heavy footsteps in the corridor outside. Jacques stood there, his hands on his hips, looking every inch the ruthless businessman who'd just threatened to take an entire company down because of a few photos. But the damage was done. They'd found her.

She scanned the room, mapping all the escape routes. They could use the secret passages and evade the police. But in her heart she knew the time for running was over. She didn't want to live the rest of her life as a fugitive. And no way could she do that to Jacques.

Grace and serenity, Maya.

"Maya Tessier, this is the local gendarme acting on behalf of the Royal Canadian Mounted Police. Come out now or we're coming in!" someone yelled from the hallway.

Maya dashed to the door and flung it open. Several police officers in full Kevlar pointed guns at her. Who knew she'd merit an entire SWAT team to take her down?

I'm a legend in my own lunchtime.

"All right, already. Keep your hats on, ladies. I'm coming," she said.

"What the hell is going on?" Jacques bellowed from behind her.

She turned and had to take a deep breath before she could look into his eyes. "It appears the Canadian government takes their subpoenas to appear in court very seriously."

"Explain." His face was rigid, the muscle in his jaw jumping radically.

"Please, Jacques. Let's go downstairs and I'll tell you everything." She pushed aside the policeman who stood at the door and headed for the stairs. She wanted Jacques's memories of his bedroom to be of the incredible joy and passion they'd experienced there. Not marred by the sludge from her past that was about to float to the surface.

At the bottom of the stairs stood a familiar face. What the hell was he doing here? Etienne was the very last person she expected to see. She'd figured he was either dead, in jail, or sipping cocktails on a beach in Rio. Were these even real cops? Her eyes darted from face to face. Ice crawled up her spine, and a scream lodged in her throat.

She scanned the uniform of the nearest police officer, looking for some sign he was legit. She wouldn't put it past Big Tony to get his thugs to pretend to be law enforcement. Etienne had obviously passed the test and was now Tony's right-hand man. How ironic that he'd be the one to come to dispose of her. Could she leverage their previous relationship and beg for Jacques's life?

Etienne spoke first and flashed a badge at her, complete with the RCMP crest. "Maya Tessier, you are under arrest for failure to appear. You have the right—"

"You're a cop?" Fear turned to rage, and the ice

in her veins became molten lava.

Etienne barely had time to nod while she launched herself at him. Before anyone could react, she slapped him hard across the cheek. Two policemen standing beside him grabbed her and shoved her arms behind her back, snapping handcuffs on her wrists.

"Now we can add assaulting a police officer and resisting arrest to your charges," one of them sneered.

"There will be no additional charges," Etienne said. "I deserved that. I have some explaining to do."

"Damn right, you do."

Princess came racing down the hall, barking loudly, her teeth bared as she skidded to a halt at Maya's side. All the cops drew their guns again and leveled them at the dog, except Etienne.

"Call off the dog, Maya. This doesn't have to get ugly," he said calmly.

"Princess, heel." She unclenched her jaw enough to make the command. She needed to keep her temper in check. The dog sat beside her but kept a wary eye on the men with guns.

Jacques pushed through the crowd and stood opposite Princess. Her two protectors. "I'm calling my lawyer," he said.

"No. Don't. Look, I'm not going to run, especially barefoot. Let's sit down and discuss this," she said. She had to keep Jacques out of her trouble.

Etienne turned to the man at his right, who appeared to be the local officer in charge. "I need to talk with the suspect for a moment alone."

"Are you sure?" the officer asked.

"Yes. We have history. She won't do anything

stupid. Will you, Maya?"

Jacques's face was ashen, his eyes haunted like he was seeing a ghost. And he was. His dreams had died again. She'd done that to him.

"No, I won't do anything stupid. But I want Jacques to come with us."

Etienne eyed up Jacques. "You trust him?"

"With my life." *And my heart.*

"Okay. Where can we talk?" Etienne asked Jacques.

Jacques nodded and led the way to his office; Princess followed. The oak-paneled room with the huge desk and comfy leather sofa had been the scene of more than one afternoon delight session. Now it would witness the end of it all.

Etienne started. "I'm an undercover RCMP officer, and I was assigned to investigate Tony Chartrand. I used you, Maya, to get into his organization. I never meant for you to get so involved. And I certainly never meant for you to witness the murders. But you did. And your testimony can send Big Tony away for good." He took a deep breath before looking into her eyes. "Maya, we need you to take a dangerous criminal off the streets and shut down his operation. We can't do this without you. Think of all the lives you'll save."

"By giving up my own?"

"We'll put you in witness protection after you testify. Give you a new identity, new life, anywhere you want."

"I don't want a new life. I like the one I have now."

"This isn't optional, Maya. You have to come."

"Why me? Can't you keep me out of this? You were there. And you're a cop, for God's sake. Your testimony is worth ten times mine."

"If I could keep you out of this, I would. But the defense is already talking entrapment and questioning my investigative methods. We need an outside, completely independent witness to corroborate my story. We need you."

"You know they're going to dig up my past— bring up Raj and Victor. I'll come off as a serial gangland girlfriend lapping up the money and expensive presents and, once my boyfriend is dead or in prison, moving on to the next thug. They're not going to take what I say seriously." She didn't have the courage to look at Jacques's face. She didn't want to see the disgust there.

"They will. The Crown prosecutor is very good. He'll have your past stricken from the record. All you have to do is tell the truth about what you saw." Etienne's voice turned soft and pleading. Like it had the time he'd begged her to go with him to Tony's cabin. Another chill ran the length of her spine.

Maya shook her head. Yeah, all she had to do was relive the worst night of her life. "You know what the kicker is in this whole effed-up situation? I was getting out of that life, and you brought me back. You dragged me back in, Etienne. And now I have to pay the price."

"I'm sorry."

"Sorry? Sorry?" She wanted to scream. She wanted to cry. She wanted to be wrapped in Jacques's arms and told this whole nightmare was over. "Sorry is what you say when you spill someone's coffee, not when you destroy their life."

Etienne had the decency to look ashamed. "You were our best bet to get into Tony's inner circle. We heard he liked you when you were with Victor. I did everything in my power to protect you. When we took down Tony, I made sure you were nowhere around. We were both arrested to keep our covers intact. And I'm protecting you now. Come back to Canada, testify, and I promise you on my badge that I'll keep you safe."

She had no choice. And really, without Jacques, what life did she have anyway? They could make her go, but they couldn't make her testify. But Big Tony had even more thugs inside prison than outside. If she were jailed for contempt of court, her life expectancy would be two days. Tops. She knew that. Etienne knew that. But it wasn't going to stop her from bargaining.

"I'll come peacefully on two conditions."

"And they are?"

"You take these handcuffs off, and you give me ten minutes to say goodbye to Jacques. Alone."

Etienne stared at Jacques again, clearly doing a threat assessment. Without a word, he pulled a key from his pocket, undid her cuffs, and walked towards the door. As he pulled it open, he turned back to them. "Ten minutes, Maya."

Ten minutes to say goodbye to the best thing she'd ever almost had.

Chapter 20

This couldn't be real. They were still in bed and he was having a nightmare. But the sick sensation was too strong to be imagined. Why hadn't she told him?

Half an hour ago she'd been warm and sensual. Now she was hard, her stance aggressive, her shoulders back, and war in her eyes. The Maya he knew, the Maya he loved, was gone. Had she been a figment of his imagination? Or a manipulation on Maya's part?

No. He wouldn't believe that.

Of all the questions bouncing through his brain, what came out was, "Did you sleep with him? Is he cupcake man?"

"No, he's not cupcake man. And I never had sex with Etienne. That should have tipped me off. A guy who didn't want my body? It was a first. I should've known he was a cop. We met when I was working in one of Big Tony's clubs. My ex, Victor, had been one of Tony's drug runners, except I didn't know that at the time. Shortly after Victor went to prison, Etienne approached me. He was kind and sweet and just listened. He came to my art shows and met me after work, drove me home, that sort of thing."

"He treated you nicely."

"Yes. Then he started hanging out at the club more, and one day he asked me to introduce him to Tony. So I did. Etienne's smart. Tony saw that and started to give him little jobs. Things started to shake up in Tony's organization. It was probably Etienne's doing. As each little guy got arrested, Etienne would take his place, until soon he was in the inner circle."

Jacques's jaw ached from clenching his teeth. Only knowing it would make things worse for Maya had stopped him from punching the undercover cop straight in the face.

Maya's voice was still hard, her stance rigid. "Our personal relationship stalled in the friends department. I liked Etienne, but I didn't want another criminal boyfriend, so I tried to break it off. I'd worked out by then that he'd only used me to get to Tony. Then Tony invited the two of us to his cabin for the weekend. Etienne begged me to go—it seemed the invitation depended on me coming as well. It's a typical gang thing. If you bring your woman, the boss has some leverage if things go wrong."

She shuddered, and he wanted to go to her, wrap her in his arms, and never let her go. But time was ticking and he had to know all of it. "What happened at the cabin?"

"It was a remote place, on a lake in the middle of nowhere. It was so dark you couldn't see your own feet. After dinner, Tony invited us all outside to view the stars. Then he shot his two closest guys. He blamed them for all the leaks and said he was cleaning house. When we got back to the city, Etienne told me it was over between us. I was angry but not heartbroken; I never loved him. The next day I went to hand in my notice at the club, but there was a raid and I was arrested. The shock of having to bail me out sent my great-grandmother into hospital.

Since I hadn't done anything except be a stupid patsy, I was released. I spent the next two weeks at Gran-Gran's side before she slipped away. She was so disappointed in me. I broke her faith, her trust, and her heart."

"Maya." His chest ached from holding in his emotions. This couldn't be happening. He couldn't be on the verge of happiness only to have it torn away again. The hope that had begun to grow in his heart shriveled and died.

"No, let me continue. I have to tell it all." She paced the floor, her hands clenched in fists. "I was devastated. Gran-Gran had been my rock, my biggest supporter. Then I heard that one of Tony's men was ready to testify and they were fast-tracking the court case. I thought maybe it was Etienne about to confess. I hadn't seen him since we were both arrested at the club. Then I was watching the news one night, and I heard a report about a murder-suicide where the man killed his whole family before taking his own life. It was one of Big Tony's guys, and I knew he'd never have killed himself, let alone his family, whom he loved. Tony had gotten to him, killed him too. Then the next night, the other witness to the original murders was found in the Saint Lawrence River. I saw the way the wind was blowing; it was my turn next. Thankfully, the lawyer handling Gran-Gran's estate had completed the transfer of the land and cottage here into my name and sent me the documents. I left the country that same evening. I wanted to put it all behind me. Start new. Make her proud of me for once."

She stopped pacing, her hands reaching out to

him for a brief second before falling to her side. "Sorry I didn't make our full thirty days. I was really looking forward to hearing your revised terms." Her voice broke, and a single tear escaped. It was his undoing.

He looked at the door then pulled her into his arms, his lips against her ear. "We can escape. I can get you out of here. I can have a plane—"

"No. It's over, Jacques." She pulled out of his arms and stood behind the chair.

If she'd shot him in the chest it couldn't have hurt more. "How can you say that?"

"Because I live in the real world. You have no idea what Big Tony is capable of. He knows I can testify against him, and he won't rest until I'm dead. I was lucky the police found me before he did. He'll have seen the pictures on the Internet, too. If I don't leave, go with the cops, he'll come after you. Or Charles or Daniel."

"I can protect us all. I have money. I can hire the best security personnel in the world."

"And we live in a compound? A prison ourselves while he goes free and kills other people? Do you know what they want me to testify about? I saw him execute two members of his gang in cold blood. He made them kneel before him and then he put a bullet in each of their heads. I can't hide anymore. I can't put other people's lives in jeopardy because I'm a coward. I have to face up to my past."

"And what about us?" Because he refused to believe she didn't care at least a little.

"I can't undo everything my great-grandmother did. I can't destroy the family she sacrificed everything to save."

"What do you mean?" His stomach clenched in knots and his chest felt like it was about to cave in.

"The real reason Gran-Gran left your grandfather wasn't because she fell in love with someone else. It was to protect your inheritance. Evidently, your family was on the verge of bankruptcy. The only thing that could save them was if Charles married some wealthy heiress. But Gran-Gran knew he wouldn't do that unless she completely broke his heart. So she did, breaking hers in the process. I now understand why she didn't come back here after my great-grandfather disappeared. Because she couldn't bear to see your grandfather married to another woman. And she wouldn't tempt him to break his vows. She never married again. She was alone at twenty-five, but she never loved again. Charles was the name on her lips when she died." Maya moved around the chair and put her hands on his face, her amber eyes brimming with tears. "And Jacques will be the name on mine when it's my time."

"Maya." The lump in his throat was so large he could barely draw air. "I can fix this. We can—"

"No. Jacques, I'm so sorry. I knew this was coming, but I was selfish. I wanted as much time with you as possible. But that time is up. I signed the sale agreement for the land; the contract is in the cottage. It's yours again. Back in the family where it belongs. I have to go. Promise me you'll look after Princess, and tell your grandfather that I love him."

"I could have Big Tony killed." He whispered the words, but they hung heavy between them.

She stepped back, out of his arms. "Then you

would become like him. And I could never be with a man who killed another in cold blood."

"I'll wait." He wasn't going to let her go.

"You don't get it, do you, Jacques? Girls like me, we're shooting stars. Shine bright and go out in a blaze of glory. Gangs have been my life. Gangs will be my death. It's over."

She strode to the door, wrenching it open. "Etienne, I'm ready to leave."

Princess gave a forlorn bark, and five minutes later, they were all gone.

***

The voices around Jacques morphed into an annoying buzz. All the CEOs of his various companies were gathered in the boardroom, presenting the last quarter's earnings reports and projected forecasts for the next year. Only one company was in deficit, and the failing venture, a tourism company, had been hit hard by the recent terrorist activity in Europe, so their drop in revenue was understandable. Altogether though, it would be another bumper year.

And it meant nothing to him. What good was a fortune when the only thing he wanted he couldn't buy?

The sale deeds that Maya signed were on his desk, but that's as far as they'd gone. He hadn't yet registered the transfer with the government. The land was back in de Launay hands. It was what he wanted. Wasn't it? The responsible thing would be to forget the past couple of months and carry on as he had before. The invisible belt around his chest tightened another notch. Screw responsibility. What had it ever done for him?

His secretary put a fresh cup of coffee in front of him before placing her hand on his arm. He glanced down. He'd written *Maya* repeatedly across the meeting agenda. When he looked up again, all eyes were on him.

What was the point in amassing more money if he had no one to share it with? Grand-Papa was recovering at home with a nurse in residence to keep him company and monitor his health. But he'd lost the spark Maya had ignited in him. They all had. And as much as it pained Jacques to admit it, his grandfather wouldn't live forever. Then Jacques would be the last de Launay.

So, he had a choice to make—continue to build his fortune and pass it on to Daniel, who didn't really need it, or some charity. Or Jacques could put on his big-boy pants and fight for what he wanted. Who he wanted. Who he loved.

Did Maya love him? Want him? Every time he closed his eyes his brain replayed the ride back from the hospital when she'd said she couldn't live like this. What had she meant? What if she only wanted his luxurious lifestyle? If he didn't have that to offer her, would she reject him? The whats and ifs were killing him, slowly destroying every vestige of sanity. How much longer could he maintain any reasonable facsimile of being in control?

He glanced down again at the agenda. Seemed his subconscious had already decided what to do.

He stood. "Thank you all for the hard work you've put into your presentations. I'd like to close this meeting with a final announcement." Everyone in the room froze. Could he really give all of it up? Could he look himself in the mirror if he didn't at least try? "I will be reducing my role as chairman of the de Launay Group. You are all eminently capable of running these companies without my oversight, and I trust you to continue to do so in my absence."

The murmur grew to a crescendo. Finally, one of the board members asked, "Jacques, are you okay?"

"Not yet, but I hope to be soon. Can anyone recommend a good tattoo artist?"

Chapter 21

Jacques slipped into the Montreal courtroom and found a place to sit on a bench at the back. He resisted the urge to scratch his new beard. *Dieu*, it was uncomfortable. But it was nothing compared to the ache in his chest. *Soon.*

Maya was led to the witness stand and all the breath whooshed out of his body. She looked … pissed off. Anger fizzed out of every pore. Even furious, she was gorgeous. More importantly, she was alive. He'd had bad dreams every night that she'd be killed before he could get to her. Before he could put his plan into action.

He'd deliberately chosen a spot where he couldn't see the defendant. Because he didn't trust that he wouldn't leap over the barrier and kill the man who threatened Maya's life.

With a cold, hard voice Maya gave her evidence, reciting the horror of that night in chilling detail. As she finished her account, a hush fell over the courtroom. Then the defense attorney stood up.

Maya's gaze swept the courtroom. It rested on him and for a split second he saw her face soften for the first time since he'd arrived. It quickly hardened again and she turned to the judge.

"I need to pee," she said.

The judge looked annoyed but called a ten-minute recess. Maya was released from the witness stand and two armed guards escorted her from the room.

Had she seen him? Had she recognized him? He hadn't quite figured out how he was going to speak to her without putting his plan in jeopardy. She was being kept in protective custody, and although he'd been in Montreal for four days, he hadn't found a way to approach her and not blow his cover. He'd shown up at the trial today because he couldn't take another day of not being near her.

When she returned to the courtroom, she had a brief word with the Crown prosecutor before returning to the stand. The defense attorney grilled her, but she remained resolute. When he brought up her past, her involvement in gang life from her teenage years, the lawyers battled back and forth with objections and the rephrasing of questions.

Finally, the judge called a recess for lunch. Jacques waited until Maya was taken out through the side door, and then he slipped out into the hallway. He put his sunglasses on and was about to exit the building when someone grabbed his arm.

"Excuse me, sir, you need to come with me."

Had Maya sent for him? The pressure in his chest eased fractionally. He followed the guard down a series of corridors to a small interview room. The door shut behind him. Endless minutes dragged on until he heard the click of heels in the hallway outside.

The noise stopped and another door opened and closed, but not into the room where he stood. He released a frustrated sigh. He turned to the mirror on the wall, sure he was being observed. Running a hand through his hair, he ground his teeth in frustration.

Court would resume in less than an hour. If Maya finished her testimony today, this would be his last opportunity to see her.

She'd said she was a shooting star. But she wasn't. She was his North Star. Without her, he was lost, directionless.

He'd almost given up waiting, about to go back to the courtroom in the hope of getting some message to her, when the door opened again and Maya walked in. She wore a baseball cap and sunglasses, but he wasn't fooled. He'd spent long enough kissing those lips to have memorized them. When they curved upward, his heart crashed against his ribs.

"What the hell are you doing here? I told you it was over," Maya said. But there was a waver in her voice.

He lifted the hat off her head and her hair spilled down her back. Next he removed the sunglasses and tossed them and the hat on the table behind him.

"Our initial thirty-day agreement is over, yes. But you said you wanted to hear my revised terms. I've come to present them," he replied. Then he kissed her. It had been six weeks since she'd walked out of the chateau in handcuffs. He wouldn't be finished kissing her anytime this year.

There was a knock on the mirror, and Maya unwrapped her arms from around his neck.

"We're being watched. And I have ten minutes before I have to be back in court. You can't be here, Jacques. If Tony gets wind of what you mean to me…"

"What do I mean to you?"

"You have to ask?"

He groaned. They didn't have time for games. "Maya, you're killing me."

She put her hand on his cheek, the gesture so familiar it hurt. "You are my world, Jacques Charles Henri de Launay. The center of my world. Everything I am spins around you. I love you so much that I'm terrified. If something were to happen to you, I wouldn't want to live."

He kissed the palm of her hand. "Excellent. That piece of information will make negotiations go a lot faster. Here are my terms. First, I am allowed to tell you as often as I want how much I love you. You may reciprocate. Second, this is an exclusive, in perpetuity agreement. You are mine and only mine, forever. Again, reciprocal. Third, you can keep the cottage and the land, but you have to change your name." He held his breath.

"What do I have to change my name to?" Her head was cocked to one side, a small smile playing about her lips. *Dieu*, he loved her.

"De Launay. And you have to marry me to do so. Those are my terms."

"I can accept terms one and two. However, it may have escaped your notice that I'm not really in a position to fulfill term three. How do you expect me to marry you when I'm under guard day and night, and the second this trial is done I'm supposed to go into the Witness Protection Program?"

"There's been a slight change of plans on that last point. When this is finished, we're both going to disappear. Big Tony will never find us and we can live happily together. My only stipulation is that you marry me first." His heart pounded as he waited for her answer. It wasn't the most romantic of proposals but the best he could do given the circumstances. He'd make up for it with the honeymoon. And the rest of their lives together.

"Wait. What? I don't understand." There was a flicker of hope in her eyes, but it was quickly doused under a wave of doubt. "You can't disappear. You're a billionaire with twenty companies to run, not to mention a world-class winery you love."

"I have people to run them for me. And even if they fail, I don't give a damn. I'd rather live in a shack with you than at the chateau alone. And I can make wine lots of places in the world. But I can't be happy without you."

"You've given up your job and your beautiful house for me?"

"Absolutely."

"What about Charles? Is he okay? I've been so worried. I'm not allowed access to the news."

"Grand-Papa is fine. He and Princess are waiting for us at our destination. He said he wanted one last adventure anyway. Personally, I think he just wants to make sure we produce the next generation of de Launays."

The hope in her eyes flared back to life. "He's not going to stand at the end of our bed and make sure we do it right, is he?"

He laughed, the first laugh in weeks. "We'll have Princess guard the door so he doesn't come in."

She put her hand on his chest and he winced. "What's wrong?"

"My tattoo hasn't healed completely yet, that's all."

193

"You got inked?"

He whipped off his leather jacket and then his T-shirt. Over his heart was the word *Maya*, the 'y' going on to form the tail of a fox.

"I got branded. And now you have to marry me, because no other woman will have me."

"Jacques, this is crazy. You can't give up your whole life for me."

"I can and I have. It's all arranged. I just need you. Will you come with me?"

"Yes."

"And marry me? I want children with you. And I want those children to be legitimate de Launay heirs. This may be the only chance we have to get married. After this, we'll be living under assumed names."

Her smile could have powered a small town. "Have you really thought this through? It could be years, or longer, before it's safe to come out of hiding. Can you live with that kind of risk?"

"I can. I've learned that life is nothing without risk. And life without you is too painful to endure. I've met your criteria for marriage. I love you, Maya. More than I thought possible to love. Marry me, please."

Her cognac eyes filled with joy. "Nothing would make me happier than to be your wife, to love you forever and have your babies."

He kissed her again, remembering her taste, the feel of her against him, and the surge of love that spread through him as she wound her fingers in his hair. His brain flashed the reminder that they were being watched, but he didn't care. Eventually, there was a rap on the two-way mirror, and he reluctantly released her mouth.

"Of all the people involved in this trial, who do you trust the most?" he asked.

"Etienne."

Jacques winced at the name. In his opinion, Etienne was the one responsible for putting Maya in this situation. "Are you sure?"

"Yes. He's feeling guilty for the position I'm in. He'll do anything to make it better."

"All right, I'll talk with Etienne. The second you're done testifying, we'll be married. Then the minute the trial is over, we're out of here."

The door flung open and the hard edge returned to Maya's face. "Time to go, Ms. Tessier," the guard said.

She turned back to Jacques as she stuffed her hair back under the ball cap. "I love you."

Then she was gone.

Chapter 22

Maya stood in the witness box doing her damnedest to remain calm. The defense attorney was deliberately trying to make her lose her cool and blurt out something stupid that he could use to discredit her. Big Tony Chartrand stared at her, and her skin crawled.

Only by concentrating on the lingering taste of Jacques on her lips did she keep her grace and serenity. A few more hours and it would all be over. Then she could spend the rest of her life making sure Jacques didn't regret his sacrifice. She still couldn't believe he'd given up his career, his home, for her.

Her eyes swept the courtroom again, but he hadn't returned after the lunch recess. She was glad, because despite the Crown prosecutor's objections, the defense attorney had dredged up her past and thrown dirt at her character, hoping something would stick and taint her testimony. She'd rather Jacques didn't hear it. If he wanted to know about her life before she'd met him, she'd tell him herself. No more secrets.

"I'm sorry. You were repeating yourself so often, I drifted off. What was your question again?" She batted her eyelashes as she spoke. The sass was back. A couple of the jurors giggled, and the Crown prosecutor hid his laugh with a fake cough.

The defense attorney, however, looked like he was about to blow. He could try to intimidate her, berate her, make her feel worthless. But Jacques loved her enough to give up his world, so she couldn't be all that bad.

"Ms. Tessier," the judge warned.

The last thing she needed was to be called for contempt of court and delay this thing any further. She answered the questions over and over, repeating her testimony word for word. Finally, the defense attorney gave up, and the judge called an adjournment until the next morning. With luck, they would be done in the next two days.

The guard escorted her out of the courtroom and through a warren of hallways into the unmarked police car that would take her to the safe house where she was staying. She'd half-expected Jacques to be waiting for her. But she saw neither him nor Etienne.

Maybe he had been present in the courtroom, in another disguise, and he'd heard all the filthy things from her past. Maybe he'd changed his mind. Six hours later, she glanced at the clock—midnight. Sleep eluded her, and the book she was reading no longer held her interest. Barred from television and Internet access, the only thing she could do was stare at the ceiling and think of Jacques.

***

The next day, the defense attorney asked for more time to pursue another piece of evidence. The judge granted a twenty-four-hour continuance, and Maya returned to her secret location.

At two o'clock she was called back to the courthouse. Had the defense attorney found something to exonerate Big Tony? Was he about to walk free? God, she hoped Jacques was ready. If he was still going through with his plan, that was.

Rather than being taken to the room where she'd previously waited to be called, the guard led her to an oak-paneled room full of books and a huge desk. One of the female Crown prosecutors, Christine, was waiting for her. "We've got fifteen minutes to get you ready for your wedding," she said.

"What?" Maya took in the rest of the room. Lying across the leather sofa was a long, white garment bag, and on the floor next to it sat a large box and the shoes she'd worn at the harvest festival.

"Your groom brought all this. I caught a glimpse of him waiting in the next room. And girl, if you don't marry him, I will."

"Not a chance. He's mine." Maya threw off her leather jacket, jeans, and T-shirt then unzipped the bag. Inside was her Gran-Gran's engagement dress, the one Maya had worn at the party. It was perfect.

She'd barely had time to fix her makeup when there was a knock at the door. Christine opened it and Jacques, Etienne, and a judge in black robes entered. Jacques was dressed in a suit, a red rose in his buttonhole. The smile he gave her settled all her butterflies. He loved her. This was real.

She repeated her vows in a firm voice, not wanting Jacques to think she had any hesitation. He promised in turn to love and care for her. When the judge pronounced them husband and wife, Jacques's kiss was so full of love, tears prickled the back of her eyes.

"You are so beautiful," he said into her ear when

he finally released her lips.

"Joe Cocker, an oldie but a goodie," she murmured back.

After they signed the paperwork, Jacques said, "I'm sorry this isn't the wedding you probably dreamed about…"

"I have the man of my dreams. For me that's more important."

He was about to kiss her again when Etienne tapped him on the shoulder. He had his cell phone in his hand and his eyes were filled with worry.

"I've got bad news. Big Tony has escaped custody. We have to get Maya to a safe location. Now."

She was already unzipping the dress and pulling her jeans back on before Etienne finished his sentence. "You got your bike here?" she asked him.

"Yes, but you'll be safer in a police car."

"And that's what Big Tony will expect. You don't think he'll have every cop car leaving the building followed? Give me the keys to your bike."

"Maya, there are protocols to be followed," Etienne said, although he dug his keys out of his pocket.

She tossed her bouquet to Christine and took Etienne's keys. Shoving her dress and shoes into the garment bag, she then handed it to Jacques. "To hell with your protocols. I'm done. You got me into this mess. I'm getting me out."

Etienne looked at Jacques, obviously seeking his support to convince Maya not to leave on her own.

"What she said," Jacques replied.

"I am so getting fired for this." But Etienne drew

his gun and led them out the door.

Eventually they arrived at Etienne's Suzuki in the underground car park. Maya handed Jacques a helmet and pulled the other on herself. "Your plane at Saint-Hubert?"

"Yes."

"Then that's where you'll find your bike, Etienne."

"I've got six cars all leaving now, heading in different directions. Good luck, Maya."

"Thanks."

Jacques got on behind her with the dress wedged between their bodies. She started the engine and, with a quick salute to Etienne, they were off.

Now, she just had to trust that Jacques's plan would work.

Maya gunned the engine the minute they cleared the parking lot, narrowly missing a car that pulled out from the curb. She fought to keep the front wheel on the ground. With Jacques's weight behind her, she had to adjust for the change in balance. Instead of holding himself stiffly as he'd done on their first ride together, he matched his movements to hers, the dress bag squished between them. She should have left it behind, but she wasn't going to let Big Tony take that one last piece of her Gran-Gran from her. Besides, it was her wedding dress now. Even a bad biker girl deserved one sentimental keepsake.

When they were away from the courthouse, she slowed down, not wanting to draw attention. She forced herself to take deep breaths and concentrate on the road, listening for other bikes or cars approaching too fast. They were almost at the small airport used by private planes when a red hatchback swerved into the lane beside them. The driver pointed a gun out the window and she slammed on the brakes, changing direction suddenly. Thank God Jacques was strong or she'd have flung him off. As it was, only by sheer determination did she manage to keep the bike under control.

Squeezing the throttle, she weaved through the cars ahead. Sirens were coming from all directions now, but she couldn't trust that the cops would get there in time. Hunkering down on the bike, she tried to make herself as small as possible, praying that Jacques wouldn't take a bullet for her. He had no protection behind him.

A trickle of perspiration dripped into her eye. Despite the sting, she kept driving as fast as she could. Jacques's life depended on her getting them to his plane in one piece. A police car waited beside the entrance to the airport, and as soon as she passed, it pulled across the road. She thought she heard gunfire but couldn't be sure as her heartbeat pounded in her ears. She concentrated on Jacques's arms around her. As long as he hung on tightly, she knew he was okay.

Two more uniformed police officers were waiting by the entrance door. Could she trust them? Did Big Tony have dirty cops on his payroll? It was a gamble, but she had no other options.

They waved her straight into the terminal building, bike and all.

"Etienne called ahead," one of them said as she shut off the bike. "Your plane is cleared for takeoff as soon as you're on board."

Maya pulled off her helmet and waited for

Jacques to do the same. He looked a little pale, but a quick check showed no bullet wounds or other injuries.

She raised her eyes to his. After this, there was no going back. She had to make sure he knew what he was in for, staying with her.

"Jacques, you can still walk away. You've seen now what being with me is like. I can't guarantee that won't happen again. Go back to France. Live free and be happy." Her voice broke on the last word.

His eyes turned fierce. "You're not getting rid of me that easily, Maya de Launay. I'm prepared to do whatever it takes to keep you safe. And if that means more wild rides with guys shooting at us, then that's what we'll do. But next time, I drive."

He passed her the garment bag, pulled two shiny new French passports out of his breast pocket, and followed the police officers leading the way to his plane. The poor rose in his lapel was crushed beyond saving.

Some wedding day.

It wasn't until they were taxiing down the runway in his Learjet that she finally took a deep breath. Then her legs began to shake so hard that they bounced up and down in front of her, out of control. The plane had barely leveled off before Jacques unfastened his seat belt and pulled her into his lap.

He hugged her so tightly, she could barely breathe. But she wasn't complaining. They'd done it. Escaped.

As his lips met hers, he whispered, "Now, where were we? Husband and wife, I think the judge said."

They kissed until the city disappeared beneath

the clouds.

"This is how to start a new life," she said when he finally released her mouth to trail kisses down to her collarbone.

Third time lucky.

Epilogue

Jacques stretched then folded his arms behind his head and relaxed into the chair. The sun was low on the horizon, a gentle breeze blew over him, and any minute now one of the staff would offer him a cocktail. But all those enjoyments had nothing on the view of Maya painting in her studio across the yard. As if sensing his stare, she looked up, a rapturous smile lighting her face. Even after almost a year of marriage, he was still enchanted.

Not for one second had he regretted giving up his life in France to live on this small winery in Chile with her. He was doing what he loved—day and night. As Maya disappeared from view, undoubtedly to wash up her brushes and join him, he turned his attention to his grandfather, who was trying to convince the gardener to shape the trees into topiary animals. Thankfully, the gardener was having none of it and insisted that trees should be shaped like trees.

Princess plodded over and flopped at his feet as if exhausted. But since her day consisted of wandering a triangle between Maya, Grand-Papa, and him, making sure each was okay or possibly harboring something to eat, he didn't think she was too tired. However, he reached down and rubbed behind her ears, earning a tail wag and a contented doggy moan for his efforts.

Maya joined them a few minutes later, bending over and giving him a kiss before taking the adjoining seat. The Andes shimmered blue in the distance, snowcapped this early in the spring. It was a bit of an adjustment getting used to the opposite seasons of the southern hemisphere. But after a restful winter, he was looking forward to a new season of winemaking.

"What are you working on today?" he asked Maya as she rubbed a foot along Princess's back.

"A special project." A mysterious smile curved her lips.

"Am I going to have to kiss the secret out of you tonight?"

Her smile got bigger. "Kissing may not be enough."

"You know how I like a challenge."

Their playful banter was interrupted by his grandfather taking the last available chair on the veranda, on the other side of Maya. If only Daniel were here, his family would be complete. But his brother was busy racing. And to keep the secrecy of their location, they corresponded only through a highly encrypted Internet cloud account.

Jacques's fingers still clenched when he recalled his and Maya's mad race from the Montreal courthouse to the airport. But it had been the right decision. They'd heard a report that the decoy police car that had been sent to Maya's safe house was under attack. He'd come so close to losing her…

She reached over and ran her hand over his fist before lacing her fingers with his. Warmth flooded through him. *Dieu*, he loved that woman.

A housemaid arrived with a tray bearing three pisco sours. "*Señor*, there is a strange ringing noise coming from your office," the young woman said as she placed the drinks on the table in front.

He exchanged glances with Maya as the color drained from her face. Only three people had the number of the cell phone he kept locked in his desk drawer—Daniel, Etienne, and her brother Sean.

"Excuse us, Grand-Papa," Maya said as she hurried after him into the house.

By the time they reached his office, the phone had stopped ringing. But it started again within a minute.

"It's Etienne," Jacques said. He swallowed down the lump in his throat. Was the RCMP officer calling to say that Big Tony had found them and that they had minutes to leave? Or was the gangster back in custody and they could now breathe easily?

"Yes?"

"Tony's dead. You can come out of hiding now," Etienne said without preamble. "We finally found him, and he was killed during the takedown. There will be no more trials. Maya is safe."

Relief swept through him. He hadn't realized how much fear for Maya's safety lingered in him until it wasn't there anymore. "Thanks, Etienne." He put down the phone and wrapped Maya in his arms. "It's over," he said against her lips. They clung to each other for several minutes. He'd have stayed incognito for the rest of his life if it meant keeping her safe.

"I guess this means we'll be returning to France now," she said when he finally released her lips.

"I don't know. I like it here, too."

"Maybe we could split our time between the two countries. Enjoy endless summer."

"You are a smart woman, Maya de Launay. *Merci à Dieu*, I don't have to remember to call you Maya Delausanne anymore. Why don't you tell Grand-Papa the good news while I call Daniel? Then we can celebrate."

She kissed him on the cheek before exiting the room. He called his brother, who, although overjoyed that they no longer had to stay hidden, had an odd catch in his voice. Something was up with him. Their first priority would be to see him at his next race.

Jacques stepped out on to the veranda, the light and clean air wiping the last of the darkness from within him. Although Chile had been their escape, it was now home. Nowhere near as grand as the chateau, but comfortable and full of love. He'd have to check on his corporations, but he wouldn't go back to working full time in Paris. He'd found his passion in a woman and winemaking.

Picking up his cocktail, he noticed that Maya had exchanged hers for a glass of fruit juice.

"At least now I'll be able to personally hang the portrait of Jacques that I'm painting in the gallery at the chateau," she said.

He froze, hope holding his tongue still.

"Those portraits are only hung when the next heir is born," his grandfather reminded them.

"Maya?" Jacques held his breath.

"Well, I vote that we should slightly amend that tradition." Maya stood and put her glass down before wrapping both arms around him. She leaned back and pure love shone from her cognac eyes. "In the spirit of equality, we should hang the picture whether it's an heir or an heiress that is born."

"Are you …?" He couldn't even say the word.

"Yup. So even if we stay here for the summer, I'd like to go to France by March. I want the first room our baby sleeps in to be in his or her ancestral home."

"That can definitely be arranged," Jacques managed to say past the lump in his throat.

A wife. A baby. A future full of love. He had it all. And he would never let go.

****

Also in the Vintage Love Series:

The Playboy and The Single Mum

He lives in the spotlight. She has to exist in the shadows.

If Formula 1 racing driver Daniel Michaud is to win the championship, he must steer clear of all distractions. But a compromising photo has his sponsor demanding that he be chaperoned for the rest of the race season. It's bad enough a sexy advertising executive is assigned to accompany him, but then they're joined by her adorable, car-obsessed son. It's all Daniel can do to keep his mind on the track and off the tantalizing taste of love and family that could destroy his career.

Lexy Camparelli blames the Formula 1 circus for her parents' divorce and the obsessive eating disorder that ruined her teenage years. To keep her job, she's forced back into that high-stakes world. At least her heart isn't in jeopardy, given Daniel's playboy reputation. Then she discovers the gorgeous driver's secret, and it's a race to see if Lexy can emerge victorious or lose everything—including custody of her son.

Visit http://alexia-adams.com to read an excerpt.

The Tycoon and The Teacher

He'll do everything he can to avoid love. It may not be enough.

Argentinian tycoon, Santiago Alvarez recently lost his sister, brother-in-law, and father. Now he's solely responsible for his traumatized niece, Miranda, who hasn't spoken for three months. His only hope to help Miranda recover is a woman who tempts him like no other. Whatever it takes, he'll live up to his promise to care for his sister's daughter—even if it means marriage.

French teacher Genevieve Dubois is slowly recovering from post-traumatic stress disorder after the death of a student. Her new position, helping a little girl find joy again, brings with it an unusual complication—a super-sexy uncle who awakens Genevieve's desire for a family of her own. When her employer proposes marriage so he can keep custody of Miranda, Genevieve accepts, hoping to turn their passion into love. But when she discovers the real reason Santiago wants to be guardian of his niece, it threatens all their futures.

Visit http://alexia-adams.com to read an excerpt.

Thank you, reader

I hope you enjoyed reading Jacques and Maya's story as much as I enjoyed writing it. If you did, please help other readers find it by leaving a review at your favorite retailer. It doesn't have to be long, but your opinion matters to me and other readers.

If you'd like to find out about other books in the Vintage Love series, upcoming releases, contests, and events, please sign up for my monthly newsletter at http://alexia-adams.com.

You can also get in touch with me via my website (http://alexia-adams.com).

I love to hear from readers, so don't be shy.

About the Author

Alexia Adams was born in British Columbia, Canada, and travelled throughout North America as a child. After high school, she spent three months in Panama before moving to Dunedin, New Zealand, for a year where she studied French and Russian at Otago University.

Back in Canada, she worked building fire engines until she'd saved enough for a round-the-world ticket. She travelled throughout Australasia before settling in London—the perfect place to indulge her love of history and travel. For four years she lived and travelled throughout Europe before returning to her homeland. On the way back to Canada she stopped in Egypt, Jordan, Israel, India, Nepal, and of course, Australia and New Zealand. She lived again in Canada for one year before the lure of Europe and easy travel was too great, and she returned to the UK.

Marriage and the birth of two babies later, she moved back to Canada to raise her children with her British husband. Two more children were born in Canada, and her travel wings were well and truly clipped. Firmly rooted in the life of a stay-at-home mom, or trophy wife as she prefers to be called, she turned to writing to exercise her mind, travelling vicariously through her romance novels.

Her stories reflect her love of travel and feature

locations as diverse as the wind-swept prairies of Canada and hot and humid cities in Asia. To discover other books written by Alexia or read her blog on inspirational destinations, visit http://alexia-adams.com or follow her on social media.

Facebook:
https://www.facebook.com/AlexiaAdamsAuthor

Twitter: https://twitter.com/AlexiaAdamsAuth

Other Books by Alexia:

Guide to Love series:

Miss Guided

Mystery writer Marcus Sullivan is determined find someone for his younger brother Liam. Playing matchmaker on holiday in St. Lucia, Marcus tries to interest Liam in beautiful local tour guide Crescentia St. Ives. Then Marcus gets stranded with Crescentia, and the plot to match her with his brother quickly incinerates in the flames of lust. No way can Liam have her when Marcus can't keep his hands off. Too bad he can't write a happier ending to their blossoming romance.

To read an excerpt visit http://alexia-adams.com

Played by the Billionaire

Internet security billionaire Liam Manning made a promise to his beloved brother, Marcus, to complete his mystery-romance manuscript. Problem is that Liam's experience with women is limited to the cold-hearted supermodels he usually dates. So falling back on his hacking skills, he infiltrates an online dating site to find a suitable woman to teach him about romance, regular-guy style. What he doesn't expect is for the feelings to be so … real. Can Liam finish the novel before Lorelei discovers his deceptions and, more critically, before she breaches the firewall around his heart?

To read an excerpt visit http://alexia-adams.com

His Billion-Dollar Dilemma

Simon Lamont is an ice-cold corporate pirate. But when he arrives in San Francisco to acquire a floundering company and is accosted by a cute engineer with fire in her eyes, it takes all Simon has to maintain his legendary cool. Helen will do whatever it takes to change his mind, and if that means becoming the sexy woman Simon didn't know he wanted, so be it. If only she wasn't about to walk into her own trap...

To read an excerpt visit http://alexia-adams.com

Romance and Intrigue in the Greek Islands:

The Greek's Stowaway Bride

Hoping to make it to North Africa to free her uncle, Egyptian heiress Rania Ghalli stows away on the yacht of Greek millionaire Demetri Christodoulou. But when Egyptian agents board the boat, she can either jump overboard … or claim she's Demetri's new bride. Demetri needs a wife to complete a land purchase, so he agrees to play along—if she'll agree to a real marriage. But keeping the vivacious heiress out of his heart will be a lot harder than keeping her on his ship...

To read an excerpt visit http://alexia-adams.com

Romance in the Canadian Prairie:

Her Faux Fiancé

Take one fake engagement to a man she once loved, stir in a very real pregnancy, add a marriage of convenience, and bake in the heat of revenge, and you get the mess that has become Analise's life.

To read an excerpt visit http://alexia-adams.com

An Inconvenient Series:

An Inconvenient Love

With the Italian economy in ruins, Luca Castellioni can't afford a distraction from running his successful property restoration company. However, he needs an English-speaking wife to cement a crucial deal. When his British bride-of-convenience undermines the foundations around his heart, he's forced to restructure his priorities. Is he too late for love?

To read an excerpt visit http://alexia-adams.com

An Inconvenient Desire

Investment banker Jonathan Davis retreats to his Italian villa to lick his wounds, so his flirtation with runway model Olivia Chapman is just that. But when his ex dumps their toddler daughter on his doorstep, Olivia's assistance is a godsend that shakes up his world in more ways than one.

To read an excerpt visit http://alexia-adams.com

Business Trip Romance:

Singapore Fling

Lalita Evans's father hired Jeremy Lakewood in the family's international conglomerate, and now he's tagging along as she oversees their interests across eight countries in three weeks. Will Jeremy risk his livelihood and all the success he's achieved to win the woman who haunts his dreams?

To read an excerpt visit http://alexia-adams.com